REVOLUTIONARY GIRL UTENA
VOL. 2: TO PLANT

This volume contains the Revolutionary Girl Utena installments from Animerica Extra Vol. 4 , No. 10 through Vol. 5 , No. 4 in their entirety.

Manga by
CHIHO SAITO

Story by
BE PAPAS

English Adaptation by
Fred Burke

Translator/Lillian Olsen
Touch-up & Lettering/Steve Dutro
Cover Design/Hidemi Sahara
Graphic Design/Carolina Ugalde
Editor/William Flanagan

Managing Editor/Annette Roman
VP of Sales & Marketing/Rick Bauer
Editor-in-Chief/Hyoe Narita
Publisher/Seiji Horibuchi

Printed in Canada.

Published by Viz Communications, Inc.
P.O. Box 77064
San Francisco, CA 94107

10 9 8 7 6 5 4 3 2 1
First printing, July 2002

ANIMERICA EXTRA GRAPHIC NOVEL

REVOLUTIONARY GIRL UTENA™

VOL. 2: *To Plant*

CONTENTS

PRONUNCIATION GUIDE:

THE "OU" SOUND IN UTENA'S LAST NAME TENJOU AND TOUGA'S NAME IS PRONOUNCED "OH" (RHYMES WITH "SNOW").

REVOLUTIONARY GIRL UTENA™

VOL. 2: To Plant

Manga by
CHIHO SAITO

Story by
BE PAPAS

ONE DAY, THE TRUTH COMES CRASHING DOWN ON A LITTLE GIRL—HER PARENTS AREN'T AWAY ON A TRIP, THEY'VE DIED. THE GRADE-SCHOOL-AGE GIRL WANDERS THE RAIN-SOAKED STREETS OF HER HOMETOWN WITH NO DISTINCT PURPOSE. DRENCHED IN RAINWATER AND TEARS, SHE FINDS HERSELF BY A RIVER, AND WITHOUT KNOWING WHAT SHE IS DOING, SHE THROWS HERSELF INTO THE ROARING FLOOD. SUDDENLY A MAN APPEARS—HER PRINCE—AND HE RESCUES HER; BANISHES HER TEARS; GIVES HER A RING ENGRAVED WITH THE MYSTERIOUS CREST OF A ROSE; AND TELLS HER TO GROW UP INTO A STRONG, NOBLE WOMAN. AND THE GIRL'S LOVE OF THE PRINCE DETERMINES HER PERSONALITY FROM THAT DAY FORWARD—SHE STRIVES, NOT TO BECOME A PRINCESS, BUT INSTEAD TO GROW UP TO BE A PRINCE JUST LIKE HIM!

SINCE THAT EVENT, UTENA RECEIVES LETTERS FROM HER PRINCE ONCE A YEAR, SCENTED WITH ROSES AND FILLED WITH ENCOURAGING WORDS. ONE SPRING, UTENA IS IN JUNIOR HIGH SCHOOL, AND HER LATEST LETTER PROCLAIMS THAT THIS IS THE YEAR SHE AND HER PRINCE WILL FINALLY MEET. ALL OF THE LETTERS, WHEN PUT TOGETHER, TELL UTENA THAT HER PRINCE IS WAITING FOR HER AT THE ELITE BOARDING SCHOOL, OHTORI ACADEMY.

UTENA ENROLLS, BUT IN THE FIRST SIX MONTHS, THERE HAVE BEEN FEW CLUES TO LEAD HER TO THE FORETOLD MEETING. AFTER WINNING A BIZARRE DUEL WITH THE STUDENT COUNCIL VICE PRESIDENT IN A SURREAL LOCATION, UTENA NOW FINDS HERSELF ROOMING WITH CLASS ODDBALL ANTHY HIMEMIYA. ANTHY KEEPS CLAIMING THAT SINCE THE DUEL, SHE AND UTENA ARE ENGAGED, AND NOW, WHILE AT STUDENT COUNCIL PRESIDENT TOUGA'S DANCE, UTENA HAS TO DEFEND ANTHY FROM HER ABUSIVE EX-FIANCÉ SAIONJI! BUT SAIONJI CATCHES UTENA DEFENSELESS AND ATTACKS HER WITH A VERY REAL SWORD!

UTENA TENJOU:
A woman striving to possess all the qualities of a noble prince.
WAKABA:
Utena's manic first roommate has been her best friend since Utena first enrolled.
ANTHY HIMEMIYA:
The mysterious "Rose Bride" is now Utena's roommate and fiancé.
TOUGA KIRYUU:
The Student Council President is also the playboy leader of the duelists.
KYOUICHI SAIONJI:
The Student Council Vice President is romantically attached to Anthy, although it seems one-sided.
JURI ARISUGAWA:
This fierce Student Council member is in love with playboy Touga Kiryuu.
MIKI KAORU:
This mild-mannered Student Council member is the youngest of the duelists.

Chapter 2:
To Plant
少女革命ウテナ
しょうじょ
かくめい

PREPARE YOURSELF, UTENA TENJOU!
I'M GOING TO DEFEAT YOU AND TAKE BACK ANTHY!

LLISH
TOUGA... KIRYUU...
Ahh! GOOD TO SEE...
...THAT THE DRESS I CHOSE ISN'T STAINED...

...JUST AN UN-FEELING PLAYBOY ...
I THOUGHT HE WAS...
MR. PRESIDENT ...?
WHY... HOW...
...DID THIS COME TO PASS?

TOUGA KIRYUU!
YOUR ARM?!
Oh, no! TOUGA!
Blood all over!
He's been hurt!
What hap-pened?

CLINIC
THEY'RE... TAKING A LONG TIME.
YES... I HOPE HE'S ALL RIGHT.
LADY UTENA...
THIS IS ALL MY FAULT.

TMP
Hmm?
BUT YOU DID NOT...
NO! HE GOT CUT BY SAIONJI IN MY PLACE!
I'D THOUGHT HE WAS JUST A PLAYBOY.
I NEVER THOUGHT HE WOULD...!
SMAAAAP
JURI? BUT WHY?

YOU CAN'T CONTINUE IN THE DUELS IF YOU GET HURT.
THAT'S WHY HE STEPPED IN!
IT'S NOT BECAUSE HE LIKES YOU, BY ANY MEANS!
DON'T YOU GO AND FLATTER YOURSELF!
WHAT WAS THAT?
DOCTOR!
WE'RE DONE IN HERE.

NOT A THING TO WORRY ABOUT.
BUT HE SHOULD REST AT THE CLINIC FOR A BIT.
CAN WE SEE HIM?
SURE.
YOU STAY OUT.
!
I AM JURI ARISUGAWA, HIGH SCHOOL SOPHOMORE...
...AND CAPTAIN OF THE FENCING TEAM.
I'LL SETTLE THIS WITH YOU-- SOONER THAN YOU THINK!

THE ROSE SEAL...
SO YOU'RE ON THE STUDENT COUNCIL...
...AND A DUELIST?

I'M NOT LIKE SAIONJI.
I WILL PREPARE MYSELF...
...TO WIN.

WHY SHOULD TWO GIRLS HAVE TO DUEL...?
SIGH
MISS UTENA TENJOU.
IT'S WRONG TO FIGHT OVER A GIRL LIKE SHE'S JUST A *TROPHY*!
I DON'T LIKE IT.
I DON'T INTEND TO CHALLENGE YOU TO A DUEL.
HEH!
I'M ALSO ON THE COUNCIL.
VVISH
I CAN'T DUEL *NOW*!

PHEW
I SEE, BUT...
I DIDN'T THINK ANYONE ON THE COUNCIL SAW IT THAT WAY...

I'M SO GLAD.
LET'S BE FRIENDS!
YOU'RE NOT A CRAZY!
GHOM
!

FUM
UM... PLEASE EXCUSE ME...
TMP

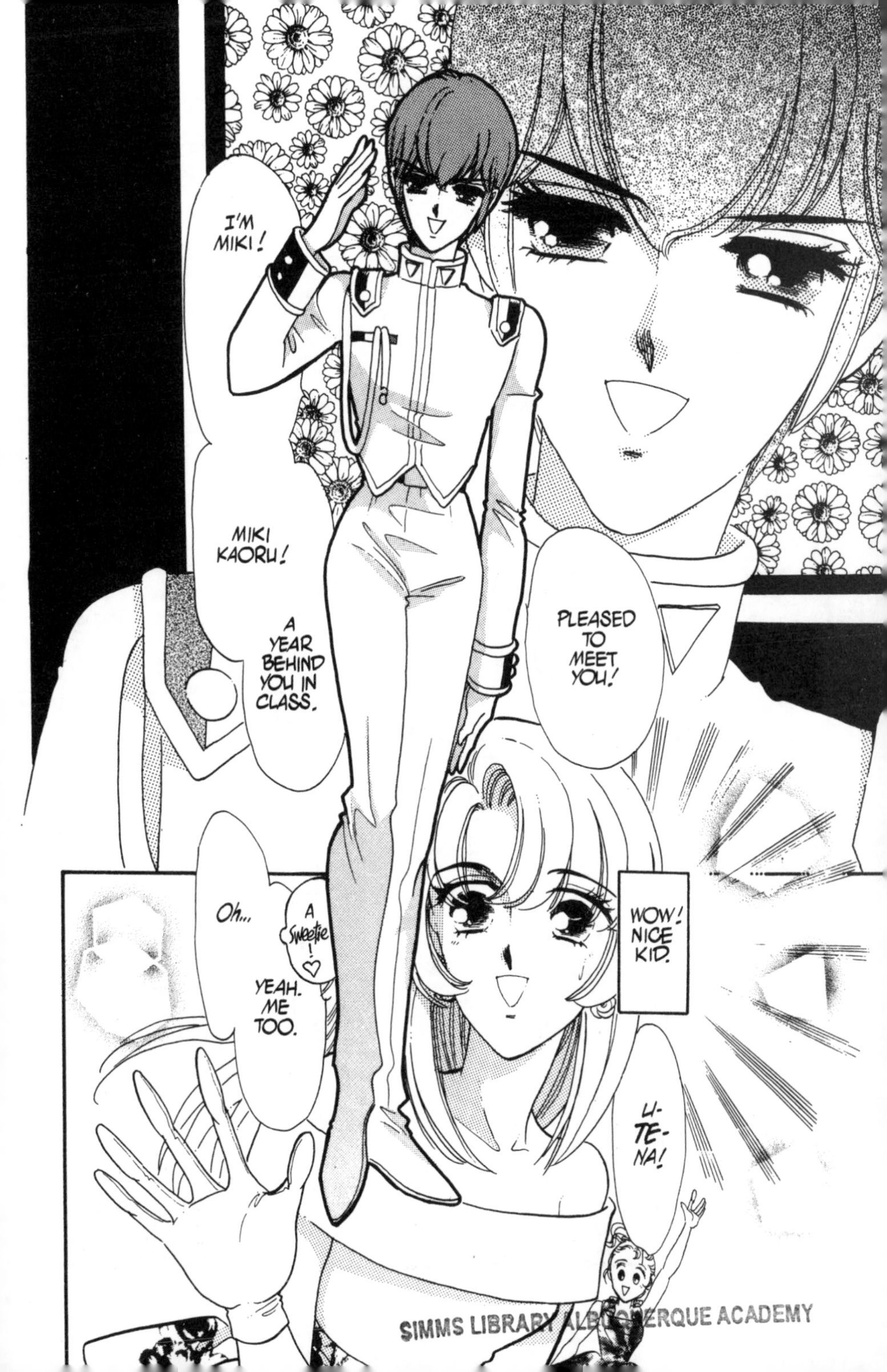

I'M MIKI!
MIKI KAORU!
A YEAR BEHIND YOU IN CLASS.
PLEASED TO MEET YOU!
WOW! NICE KID.
A Sweetie! ♡
Oh...
YEAH. ME TOO.
U-TE-NA!

WHSH
HUH?
BONG
I GOT WORRIED WHEN I HEARD THE PRESIDENT GOT HURT, SO I CAME OVER.

THAT WAS...
MICKY FROM THE STUDENT COUNCIL.
DO YOU KNOW HIM?
UTENA! DID YOU SEE THAT?

AND HE'S TAKING COLLEGE CLASSES IN JUNIOR HIGH!
BUT HIS FENCING AND PIANO PLAYING-- NATIONAL LEVEL!
HE'S SO PRETTY AND NICE...
WOW!
THE OLDER GIRLS ARE ALL OVER HIM!
GET A CLUE!
YOU CALL HIM MICKY?
What the heck?

HE AND ARISUGAWA ARE CLOSE.
SHE'S THE CAPTAIN OF THE FENCING TEAM AND A COUNCIL MEMBER.
THEY'RE FAMOUS AS THE HANDSOME DUO!
SEE... MICKY'S SO NICE...
...WHILE SHE SCARES EVEN THE TEACHERS!
THEY CALL HER "THE BEAUTIFUL LEOPARD" BEHIND HER BACK!
WHAT A PAIR, huh?

LADY UTENA, I BROUGHT YOU A CHANGE OF CLOTHES.
BUT WHY...?
LIKE SHE HATED ME FROM THE START...
BUT IN ANY CASE...
I SEE.
...THAT SLAP OF HERS HURT-- A LOT.
LET ME HELP YOU UN-DRESS.
ANTHY HIMEMIYA?
HEY! WHAT IS--
BUT... I BELONG TO LADY UTENA?
WHAT ARE YOU DOING TO MY UTENA?
Oh, GREAT.
I SAID, I belong to...
Say that again!
WHAT DID YOU SAY?

CLINIC
I WAS LUCKY. IT'S NOT A SERIOUS WOUND.
DIDN'T YOUR USUAL PICKUP LINES DO THE TRICK, TOUGA? DID YOU REALLY HAVE TO RESORT TO CHIVALRY?
RUBBISH. YOU TOOK YOUR ARM OUT OF COMMISSION FOR THREE MONTHS, JUST FOR THAT GIRL?
AND ONCE YOU'VE HAD HER, YOU'LL THROW HER AWAY, RIGHT?

TWO WEEKS!
I CAN'T AGREE TO THAT.
TWO WEEKS SUSPENSION, KYOICHI SAIONJI...
...FOR INJURING THE COUNCIL PRESIDENT, TOUGA KIRYUU.

WHY NOT?
TOUGA BUTTED IN DURING *MY* DUEL.
HE BROKE THE RULES.
MY FIGHT WAS WITH UTENA TENJOU.
THIS WAS *HIS* FAULT.
THAT'S NOT TRUE, MR. VICE PRESIDENT.
YOU'RE THE ONLY ONE WHO CALLS THAT A DUEL.
IT WASN'T AT THE DUELING GROUNDS. AND WHERE WAS THE ROSE BRIDE, OR THE SWORD OF DIOS?
Hmph.
DON'T BE SO SELF-RIGHTEOUS, LITTLE PRODIGY!
DO YOU HAVE ANYTHING ELSE TO SAY?

WHAT RIGHT DO YOU HAVE...
...TO DECIDE THIS ABOUT ME, THE VICE-PRESIDENT?
TOUGA GAVE ME THAT RIGHT...
...WHEN HE TOOK AWAY YOUR OFFICE!
YOU ARE VICE PRESIDENT NO LONGER!

BUT TOUGA PROTECTED UTENA TENJOU ON HIS OWN.
NO. HE WAS PROTECTING THE RULES OF THE ROSE SEAL AS STUDENT COUNCIL PRESIDENT...
HE WAS NOT!
HE DID IT BECAUSE HE LIKES UTENA TENJOU-- WANTS HER!

RIDICULOUS... TOUGA MAY BE QUICK WITH WOMEN, BUT HE DOESN'T FALL IN LOVE WITH THEM.
THIS TIME HE HAS.
IF HE STEPS IN WITHOUT THINKING...
THEN I SAY HE'S SERIOUS ABOUT HER.
YOU MAY LOVE HIM...
...BUT I'VE KNOWN HIM SINCE CHILDHOOD!
I'LL QUIETLY STAY IN MY DORM ROOM, SUSPENDED.
I SUGGEST YOU KEEP YOUR EYE ON UTENA TENJOU.
KLIK

CLINIC
MAYBE THIS IS TOO MUCH...
WILL HE LAUGH AT ME?
WHAT'S THAT?
I SEE...
YOU BROUGHT HIM *FLOWERS*...

TO PLANT

HA HA HA HA HA HA
Um...
I JUST WANTED TO...
SAVE IT...
FWNK
TRASH
TOUGA GETS ENOUGH FLOWERS EVERY DAY TO START A COMPOST HEAP.
But that was..
WHY IS SHE SO MEAN TO ME?
GO, U-TE-NA!
SLAM A HOMER!
WHOOO
JUST WATCH ME!

YO, JURI!
HOW ABOUT A LITTLE PRACTICE MATCH?
CLASH
SMASH
OVER THERE-- IT'S UTENA.
SHE AMAZES ME.
SUCH ATHLETIC SKILL.
SHE TOOK ON SAIONJI, THE KENDO CAPTAIN...
...SO I BET SHE COULD EVEN FENCE.
SOUNDS LIKE SHE'S BEAT YOU ALREADY.
WHAT?

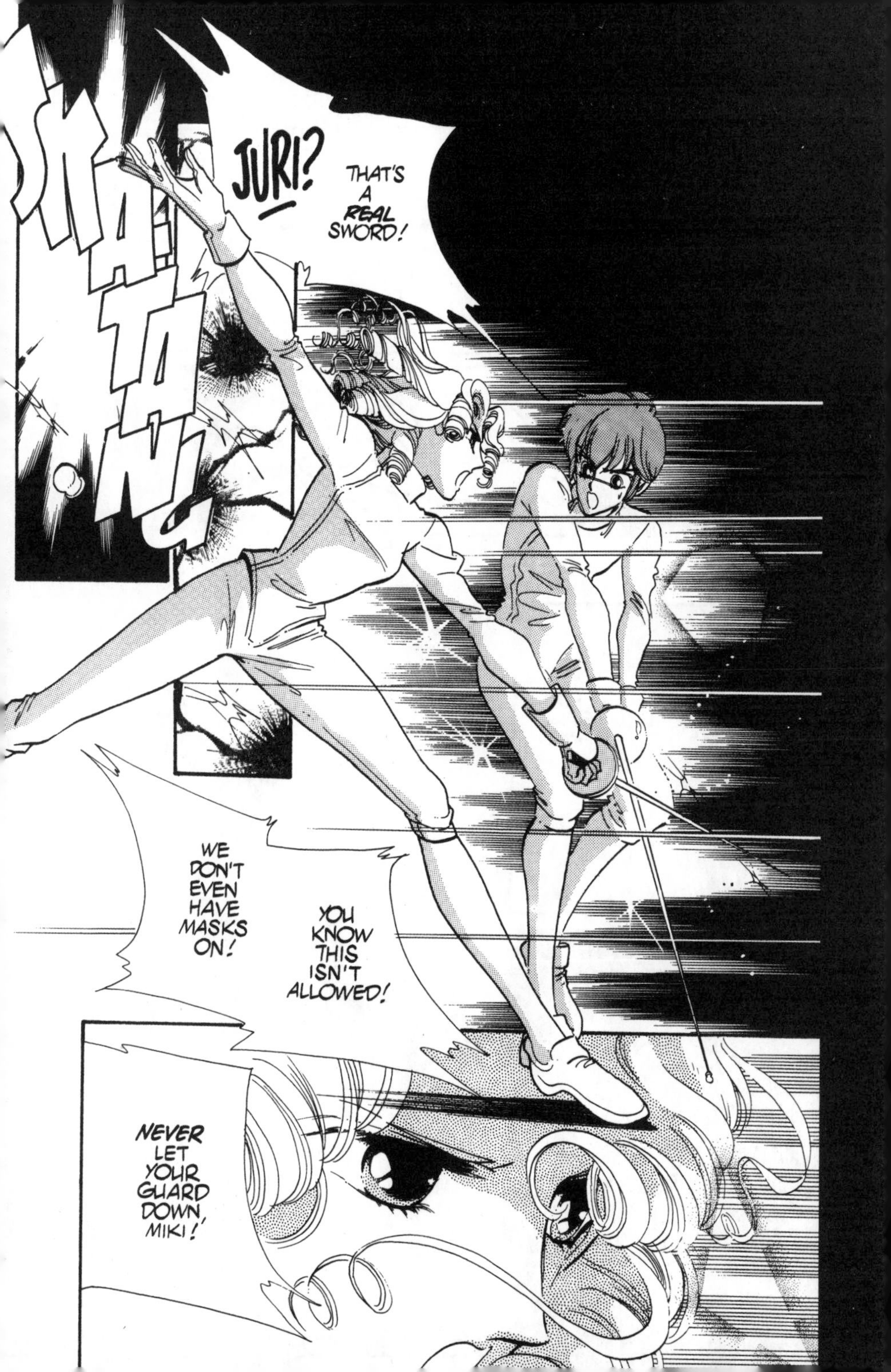
THAT'S A REAL SWORD!
JURI?
YOU KNOW THIS ISN'T ALLOWED!
WE DON'T EVEN HAVE MASKS ON!
NEVER LET YOUR GUARD DOWN, MIKI!

JURI! WATCH OUT!
...JURI...
IT WAS A FOUL BALL AND...
SORRY!

Heh.
SHE STABBED IT OUT OF MID AIR.
AHH
WOW...
FWIP
SHE'S-- AMAZING!
JURI ARISUGAWA ...

YOU KNOW, ANTHY...
...I CAN'T HELP BUT FEEL ARISUGAWA IS PICKING ON ME.
EAST HALL
.....
MY!
EVERY DAY A NEW SLIGHT.
LIKE TODAY, SHE FLIPPED MY LUNCH OVER IN THE CAFETERIA.
OH, NO. REALLY?
STCH
AND SHE CALLED ON ME IN MORNING MASS AND MADE ME SING A SOLO.
I can't sing.
THAT'S JUST AWFUL.
Your turn, Chuchu.
Chu.

WHY YES. OF COURSE I AM, LADY UTENA!
ANTHY, ARE YOU EVEN LISTENING TO A WORD I SAY?

SO...
...IT'S JUST AS I FEARED...
...THIS "BEAUTIFUL LEOPARD" IS AFTER ME!
URGH
DO YOU MIND?
AND I'VE SEEN IT ALL BEFORE. ONE DAY SOON, ARISUGAWA WILL CHALLENGE YOU TO A DUEL.

I'M IN THIS GAME--FOR GOOD.
I'LL DO WHAT I MUST...
...WHEN THE TIME COMES.
NO. NOT REALLY.

BUT ANTHY, YOU'RE A GIRL...
WHY DOES JURI WANT YOU?
IT'S NOT THAT.
THERE ARE ALWAYS OTHER REASONS.

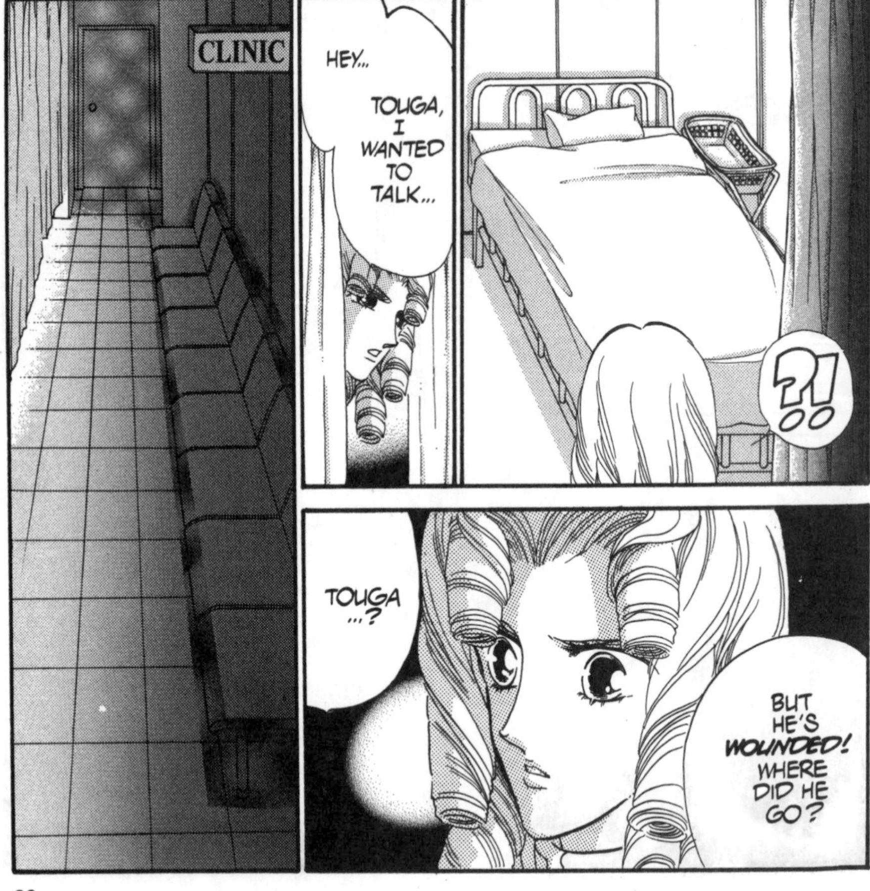

CLINIC
HEY...
TOUGA, I WANTED TO TALK...
?!
TOUGA ...?
BUT HE'S WOUNDED! WHERE DID HE GO?

MM...
Chu.
Chu.
Chu Chu!

GRRR!
...WHA?
Chu
Chu
WHAT'S WRONG WITH YOU, CHUCHU?
Chu

TOUGA KIRYUU!
I THOUGHT YOU WANTED TO HEAR ABOUT "WORLD'S END." I SAID I'D TELL YOU...
DON'T MESS WITH ME.
I HAD TO COME AND SEE YOU.
WHAT ARE *YOU* DOING THERE? SHOULDN'T YOU BE IN BED?

COME DOWN, UTENA.
LET'S WALK TO THE DUELING FIELD.
I WANT TO SHOW YOU SOMETHING.
IS HE REALLY SERIOUS?
COME ON...
WHAT COULD BE AT THE DUELING FIELD?
"WORLD'S END," MAYBE?
...JUST WAITING FOR US?
OH...

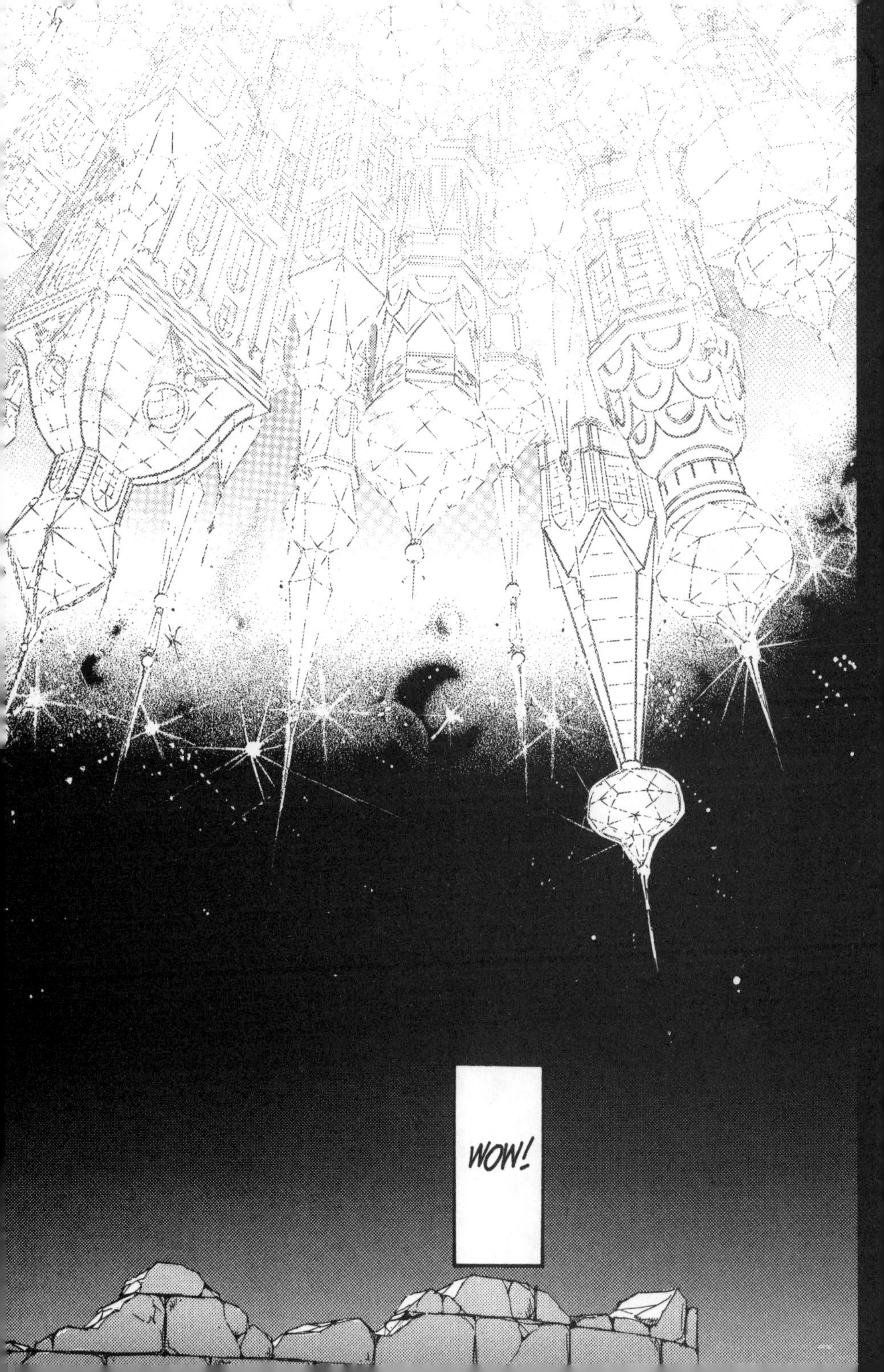
WOW!

SEE...?
IT'S DAZZLING...
IT-- IT'S LIKE...
...A CHANDELIER.
BUT I WANTED YOU TO SEE IT AT NIGHT... WITH ME...
YOUR WOUND... YOU'VE WORN YOURSELF OUT. YOU SHOULDN'T TAKE SUCH CHANCES.

I... I SEE.
I'M SORRY YOU GOT HURT PROTECTING ME.
IT WAS KIND OF YOU.

BUT THAT'S A KNIGHT'S DUTY, ISN'T IT?
A KNIGHT IS ALWAYS PREPARED TO THROW DOWN HIS LIFE TO PROTECT THE PRINCESS.

BUT THAT'S WHAT I DON'T TRUST ABOUT YOU... NO OFFENSE.
SHU
BESIDES... I DON'T WANT TO BE A PRINCESS. I WANT TO BE A PRINCE! NO OFFENSE.
A PRINCE? WHY?

IT'S A STORY THAT DOESN'T FIT ME AT ALL.
YOU'LL LAUGH.
.....

I'D LIKE TO HEAR IT, WHILE I'M RESTING HERE, IF YOU DON'T MIND...
"DOESN'T FIT"? THAT MAKES ME MORE CURIOUS...

.....

I WAS SIX...
...WHEN MY MOM AND DAD DIED...
...AND I DIDN'T KNOW WHAT TO DO.
I WANDERED ALL OVER TOWN AND, ON A BRIDGE, I ALMOST **FELL**...
IT WAS **THEN**...
...THAT A PRINCE SAVED MY LIFE.

HE GAVE ME THIS RING AND HE TOLD ME...
"THERE WILL COME A TIME WHEN WE MEET AGAIN...
...IF YOU DO NOT LOSE..."
"...YOUR NOBLE HEART..."
A GOOD REASON TO WANT TO BECOME A PRINCE.
HOW DID HE KNOW?
...
THOSE WORDS--ONLY THE PRINCE AND I KNOW THEM!
STRENGTH, NOBILITY, PASSION... THE THINGS THAT MAKE US GREAT.
ONLY THOSE WHO HAVE NOT LOST THEM CAN EVER REACH THAT CASTLE IN THE SKY.

THE ANSWER TO EVERY MYSTERY...
...AND THE POWER OF DIOS...
EVERYTHING IS IN THAT CASTLE.
NO WAY...
IT CAN'T BE...
WHEN THEY ARE YOURS...
...THEN YOU WILL BECOME THE PRINCE THAT YOU DESIRE.
...COULD IT...?
IT COULDN'T BE HIM...

UTENA TENJOU!
MY PRINCE ...

AS I FEARED...
...THE TIME HAS COME...
I INVITE YOU... ...TO A DUEL!

GONG GONG
GONG GONG
JURI ARISUGAWA, THE FENCING TEAM CAPTAIN...
"BEAUTIFUL LEOPARD" INDEED!
GULP
Ah, UTENA TENJOU! THERE YOU ARE!

A DUEL...
.....
THE SMALL ROSE WITHIN ME...

...WITH HER...
MY CLOTHES...
HUH...?
...FOR YOU...

ANTHY...
THE ROSE THAT TAKES FLIGHT...
...FROM WORLD'S END.
A GIFT-- FOR YOU...
ANTHY... IS THIS... IS THIS MORE MAGIC?

STUDENT COUNCIL PRESIDENT... AND MIKI... YOU'RE HERE, TOO.
THAT'S THE DRESS UNIFORM.
THE DUEL IS A SACRED RITUAL AFTER ALL...

ARE YOU...
...THE PRINCE I'VE BEEN SEEKING?
I WISH I COULD ASK HIM, BUT...
SO YOU KNOW THE RULES OF THE DUEL?
SWIP

FROM THAT TIME...
...SHOW NOT YOUR FACE...
...TO EITHER THE ROSE BRIDE OR TOUGA. NOT EVER.
THE ONE WHOSE ROSE GETS KNOCKED OFF LOSES.
YES... I KNOW.
LET'S GET ON WITH IT.
FINISH
OKAY. I WILL.
PLEASE... BE CAREFUL.
FOR ME...

SWORD OF THE ROSE...
...THE POWER OF DIOS THAT SLEEPS WITHIN ME...
...ANSWER TO YOUR MASTER--
--AND SHOW YOURSELF NOW!

IT'S SO BRIGHT...
...SO I CAN'T SEE HOW THIS WORKS.
BUT I SEEM TO RECALL...
...THAT IT WENT SOMETHING LIKE THIS...

GRANT POWER TO MY SWORD...
THE POWER TO REVOLUTIONIZE THE WORLD!

NOW!
KATANG
HAH!
HAH!
KATANG
KLANG

...NO WONDER THEY CALL HER "THE BEAUTIFUL LEOPARD"!
HER GUARD IS SO TIGHT...
IS THAT ALL YOU HAVE?
WHAT'S THE MATTER, UTENA TENJOU?!
TMPTMPTMPTMP
WAM
ZZZT

AND YOU WILL STAY AWAY FROM TOUGA!
I WILL WIN-- YOU HEAR ME?
Unh...
WHOSE SIDE ARE YOU ON?
JURI'S GOOD.
UTENA TENJOU MIGHT LOSE.
SO I CAN'T LOSE.
HAVE TO ASK TOUGA...
HAVE TO KNOW...
I... I WON'T LOSE-- NOT YET...!

S- SOMETHING'S COMING DOWN-- FROM THE CASTLE!
WHAT ?
FWASHHHHHHH

THERE IT IS...
THE SCENT OF ROSES, LIKE BEFORE.
WHAT ...?
SHAAA
HE HAS COME... DIOS.

AS IF I WAS FLOATING...
...FLOATING IN A CLOUD OF ROSES...

Y-
YOU!
YOU WON'T FOOL ME WITH YOUR TRICKS!
!
I CAN SEE-- SEE IT ALL!
EVERY ONE OF HER MOVES... CLEAR TO ME!

M... MY...
...ROSE...

UTENA TENJOU IS THE WINNER.
NOOOO!
BUT HOW? NO IDEA WHAT HAPPENED...
I--I WON?
IT WAS YOUR ERROR, JURI.
YOU LET DOWN YOUR GUARD.
IT WAS A TRICK!
THAT THING CAME DOWN ALL OF A SUDDEN...
AND... AND I...
SO THAT IS WHAT WE CALL DIOS...
I'VE NEVER SEEN IT BEFORE.

BUT IT'S NOT FAIR...
DON'T DISGRACE YOURSELF.
IF YOU DON'T LIKE THE OUTCOME, CHALLENGE UTENA TENJOU TO ANOTHER DUEL.
JURI?
!
THAT WAS TOO HARSH!
YOU KNOW HOW SHE FEELS ABOUT YOU...
THERE'S...
SOMETHING I HAVE TO ASK YOU!
I CAN'T HELP BUT THINK...
...THAT MAYBE, WELL--AREN'T YOU THE ONE?
MY PRINCE?

HE--HE ONLY HAS EYES FOR THE CASTLE ABOVE...
NO ROOM INSIDE HIM... FOR ANYTHING ELSE.

HTOR
MY AIM IS OFF...
...MY MIND'S ON OTHER THINGS.
OOOOOOH
YOU CAN DO IT!
GO FOR IT!
THUD
CAN'T SEEM TO *STOP...*
JUST KEEP THINKING HOW TOUGA KIRYUU LOOKED THAT DAY...

UTENA!
YOUR GIRLFRIEND WAKABA IS ROOTING FOR YOU!
SO SHAPE UP!

WHSH
SORRY... I'M NOT IN THE MOOD TODAY.
UTENA?
WHAT'S UP WITH YOU?
YOU'VE BEEN ACTING WEIRD EVER SINCE YOU MOVED IN WITH ANTHY HIME-MIYA.
WHAT DID SHE DO TO YOU?
NO, IT'S NOT THAT.

BUT...
STOP BEING SILLY, OKAY?
REALLY-- THANKS FOR YOUR CONCERN, WAKABA.
UTENA...
Sigh

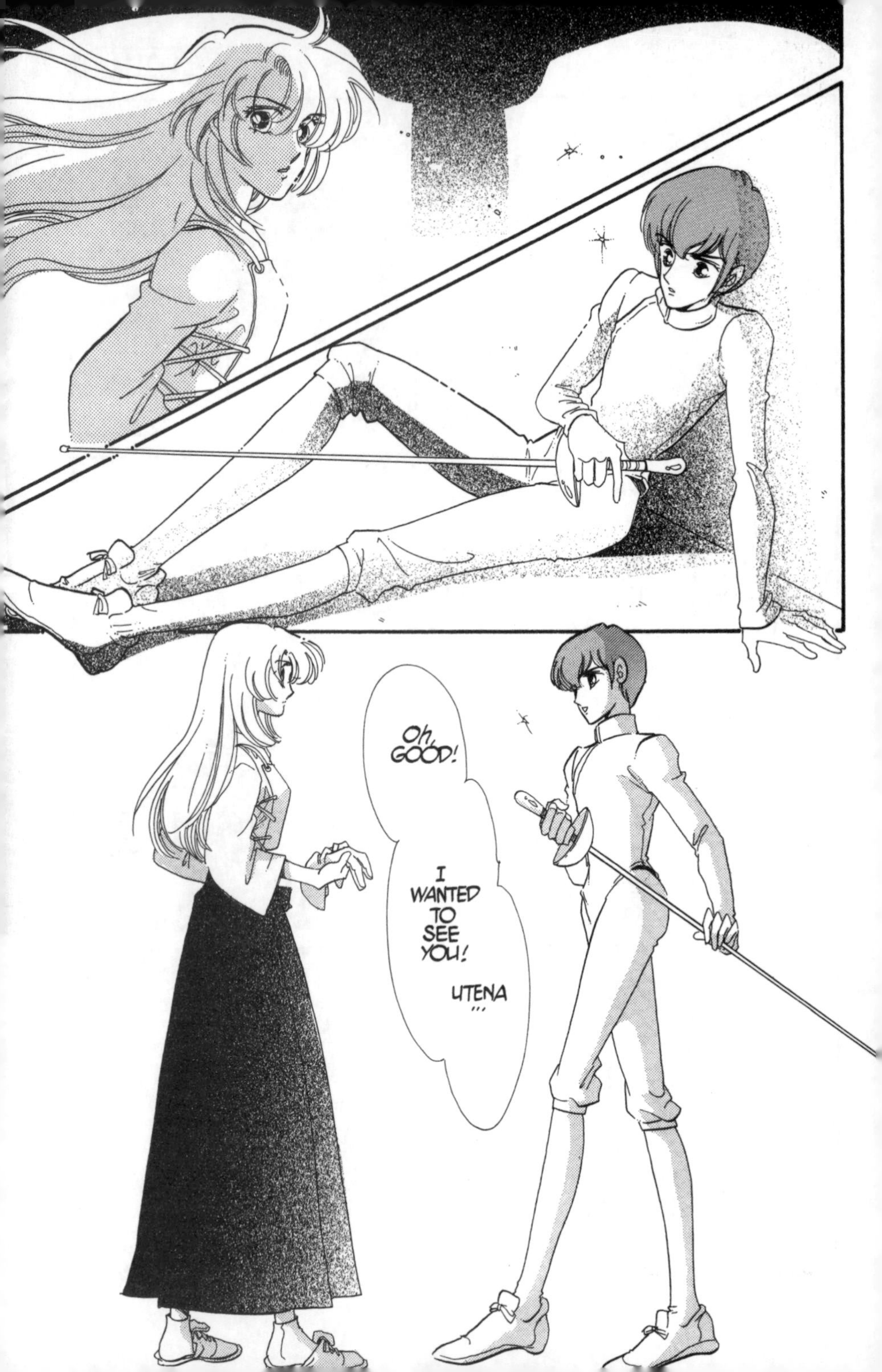
Oh, GOOD!
I WANTED TO SEE YOU!
UTENA ...

STUDENT COUNCIL, FENCING-- I'VE BEEN ABLE TO STICK IT OUT... BECAUSE SHE WAS THERE...
JURI'S DONE SO MUCH FOR ME.
I FEEL SO SORRY FOR HER.
IT'S JUST NOT LIKE HER-- SHE'S ALWAYS BEEN SO TOUGH...
JURI'S BEEN SO DOWN OF LATE.
WHY CAN'T HE SHOW HER A LITTLE COMPASSION?
WE'RE ALL SUPPOSED TO BE FRIENDS.
BUT THIS THING WITH TOUGA IS TEARING HER UP!
Huh?
SO YOU'LL COME SPY ON TOUGA WITH ME, RIGHT?
UTENA, THAT'S GREAT!
I THINK YOU'RE RIGHT.
YOU KNOW...

WE'RE IN THE CLEAR!
HE SHOULD STILL BE AT THE CLINIC.

THIS IS TOUGA KIRYUU'S DORM ROOM?
HE LIVES HERE BY HIMSELF? WOW!
The polar opposite of my dorm.
THEY CALL IT THE WHITE HOUSE.
THE STUDENT COUNCIL PRESIDENT OF OHTORI ACADEMY MIGHT AS WELL BE THE PRESIDENT...
...WITH ALL THE SPECIAL PERKS HE'S GIVEN.
YOU KNOW...
...HE COULD TAKE ADVANTAGE OF THAT TO PLOT SOMETHING...
Umm...
...UTENA?

WE *CAN* JUST USE THE FRONT DOOR.
DOH
JUST TO MAKE IT EASY...
...I "BORROWED" THE KEY FROM HIS LOCKER.
Hmph.
YOU GET A KICK OUT OF THIS, *huh?*
OF COURSE!
HE WOULDN'T TELL ME IF I ASKED.
SO IT'S HIS OWN FAULT.
Yep.
BECAUSE IF I INVESTIGATE TOUGA KIRYUU'S *SECRETS*...
...I *COULD* FIND OUT IF HE'S MY PRINCE OR NOT.
UTENA, CHECK IT OUT!

IT LOOKS LIKE THIS IS HIS ROOM.
THERE MUST BE A CLUE HERE.
NOW I CAN FINALLY SEE WHAT KIND OF PERSON HE IS...
...TOUGA KIRYUU.
THE REST OF US...
...WE JUST RECEIVE LETTERS FROM WORLD'S END... THE SHORTEST OF MESSAGES.
SHPP

BUT HE GETS MORE.
I HAVE THE FEELING, STANDING HERE, THAT HE'S ACTUALLY IN TOUCH WITH WORLD'S END.
JUST A FEELING, BUT A STRONG ONE.
YOU KNOW?
LIKE HE KNOWS THINGS WE DON'T...
...DOES THINGS IN SECRET.
OF COURSE! THAT'S BECAUSE...
...HE'S THE PRINCE...
Huh?
Oh, um... NOTHING.

WHAT'S THIS...?
Oh... THAT'S TOUGA'S SISTER.
SHE'S IN SEVENTH GRADE HERE.
HOW SWEET! SHE'S SO PRETTY!
IT MUST BE NICE TO HAVE SIBLINGS.
I'M AN ONLY CHILD...
I ENVY THAT, YOU KNOW?
I...
I HAVE A SISTER, TOO.
WE'RE TWINS.
YOU ARE?
IS SHE CUTE LIKE YOU?
CU...
BLUSH

Oh, SORRY.
DID I HIT A SORE SPOT?
I'M SO DENSE.
.....
...NO.
IT'S OKAY... WITH *YOU*.
...YOU SEE, I...
WITH *YOU* I CAN TALK ABOUT ANYTHING. I...
MM?
WHEN HE GAZES AT ME...
...THOSE DEEP EYES SHINING...

CLICK
TMP
TMP
TMP
HE... HE CAME HOME?
Oh, NO!
LET'S HIDE.
WH...
THE CLOSET!
SHAEEEE
HUH?

FVUMP
...OW.
ARE YOU OKAY?
Y... ...YEAH. YOU?
I GUESS THIS ISN'T JUST *ANY* CLOSET.
PADOOOM
UTENA... IS THIS FOR *REAL*?
I SEE IT, TOO.
WH-- WHAT *IS* THIS PLACE?

TOUGA'S SECRET! A HIDDEN STUDY OF SOME KIND!

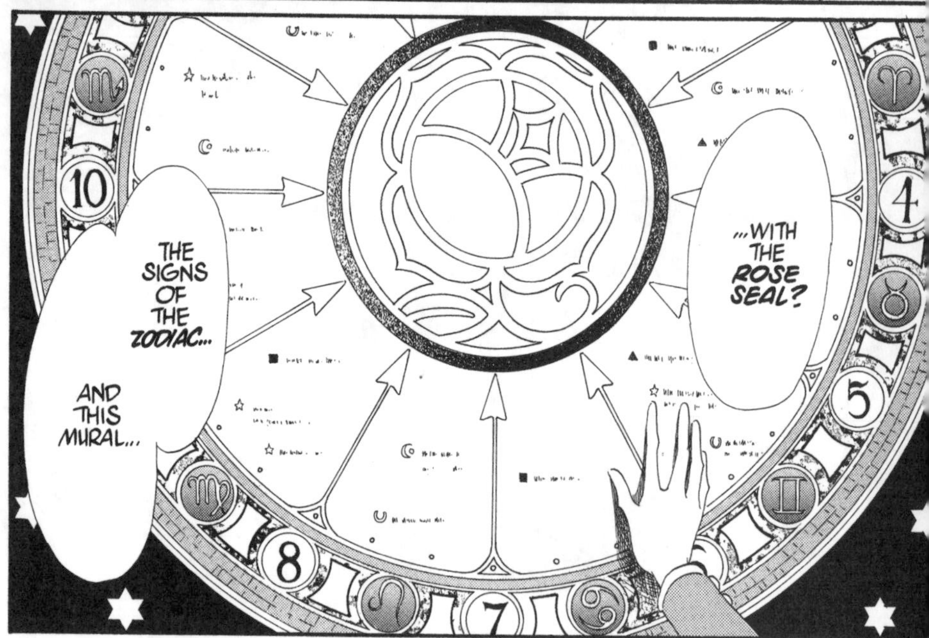
...WITH THE ROSE SEAL?
THE SIGNS OF THE ZODIAC...
AND THIS MURAL...

.....
IT'S SOME KIND OF CALENDAR.
—Yeah.
LOOK, WRITTEN IN HERE...
...SYMBOLS AND MEMOS.
A SCHEDULED DUEL...?
.....
WHAT?
INFORMATION ABOUT THE DUELS!
IT'S ALL WRITTEN ON THIS CALENDAR.
IT IS?
THE DUEL BETWEEN YOU AND SAIONJI LAST MONTH...
THE DUEL WITH JURI THE OTHER DAY...
ARE YOU SURE IT'S NOT JUST A RECORD OF WHAT HAPPENED?

WHY WOULD *WE* DUEL?
THAT'S BOGUS.
YES! I MEAN ...
I WON'T DO THAT.
I WON'T DUEL-- AND NOT WITH *YOU!*
YOU SAY THAT *NOW!*
BUT... YOU WILL, MIKI. YOU *WILL!*
!
NO... IT SAYS THAT...
IT SAYS THAT YOU AND I WILL DUEL NEXT MONTH...
DUEL WITH YOU?

IT NEVER FAILS.
NOT ONLY THAT! YOU WILL WANT TO...
TOUGA KIRYUU...
HOW WOULD HE KNOW...?!

MIKI KAROU ...
...YOU WILL...
...WANT TO DUEL!

IT NEVER FAILS...

YOU WON'T! AT LEAST...
...THAT'S WHAT I'D THINK!
IF YOU LIKE HER, EVEN A LITTLE... YOU WON'T LET HER DO IT!
DON'T YOU FEEL FOR UTENA?
SOMETHING SO DANGEROUS? HOW CAN YOU JUST SAY THAT?
.....
TOUGA!
BECAUSE I CAN'T DUEL!
I'LL PROTECT THE GIRL I LOVE!

MIKI...
WHMP
UNGH!
CAN'T YOU SEE THAT?
UTENA ISN'T HERE TO BE PROTECTED.
I JUST CAN'T...
...STAND IT ANYMORE!
I REQUEST THE DISBANDMENT OF THE STUDENT COUNCIL!
WE CAN'T FOLLOW SUCH INHUMAN RULES!

SHHA
K-KIRYUU? W-WHAT...
...ARE YOU GOING TO DO WITH UTENA?
BAM
BAM
LET ME IN!
BAM
BAM
THE WONDERFUL WIZARD OF OZ
TO PROTECT...
...IS TO LOVE?
Ah...!
IS THAT WHAT YOU THINK?
SO NAÏVE, MIKI.

A GOOD QUESTION.
WHAT SHALL I DO?
WHA...?
PADOOM
W-WILL HE FORCE HIMSELF ON ME...
...LIKE LAST TIME?

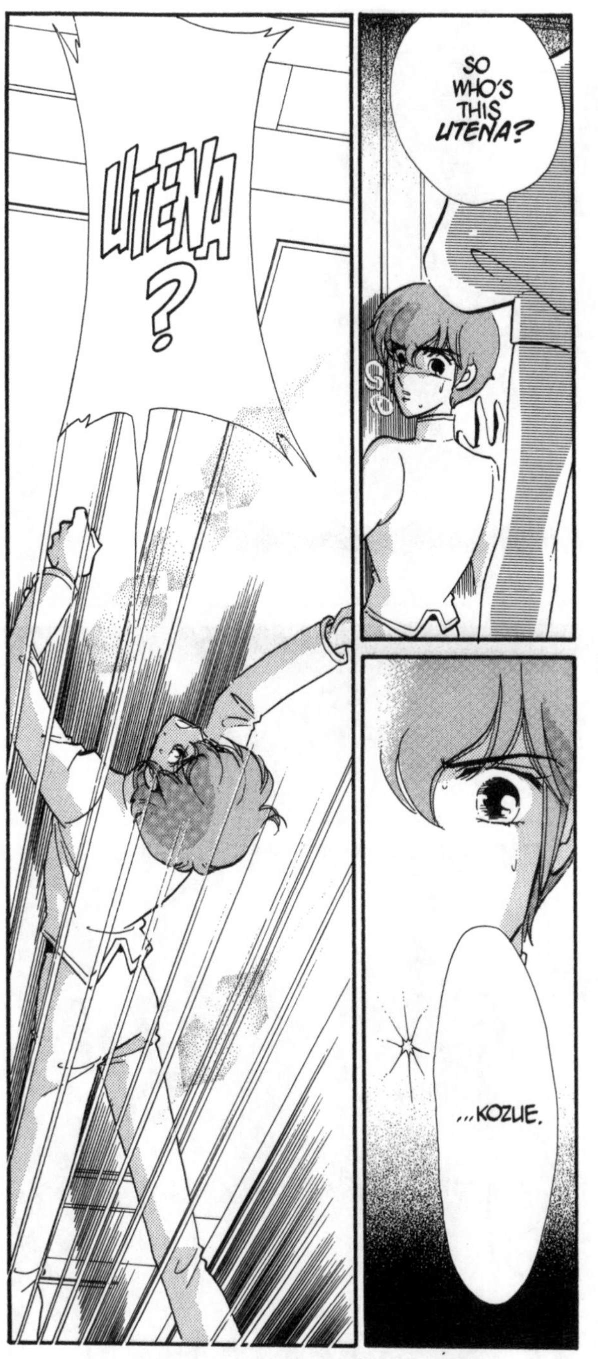

TEAM UTENA MEMBER NUMBER 0

CHUCHU

AGE: CHU(???)
BIRTHDAY: CHU!
ZODIAC SIGN: MONKEY!

BLOOD TYPE : MONKEY!

HEIGHT:
BETWEEN 10CM(4")
AND 50CM(20"). (???)

HOBBY:
EATING!

TALENT:
I CAN EAT
ANYTHING!

DISLIKES:
-WHEN I EAT SOMETHING AND IT TASTES BAD!
-WHEN I EAT SOMETHING AND IT ISN'T FOOD!
-KYOUICHI SAIONJI
(JUST NOT A TASTY GUY)

TOUGA...
IS **OUR** DUEL PLANNED, TOO?
HAVE YOU PUT IT IN YOUR CHART...

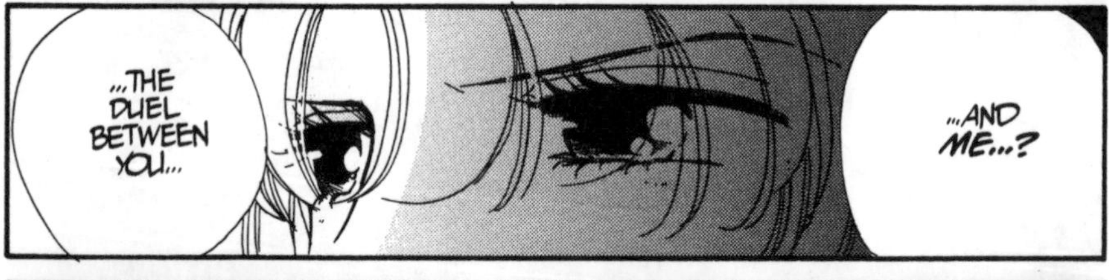
...THE DUEL BETWEEN YOU...
...AND **ME**...?

ERFUL WIZARD OF

IF YOU BREAK AND ENTER AGAIN...
...I WON'T LET YOU OFF SO EASY.
NOW GO...
I'LL...
I'LL BE WAITING FOR YOU TO GET **STRONG.**
SLAM
WH-WHAT WAS THAT ABOUT?
PAPOOM PAPOOM PAPOOM

UTENA! ARE YOU ALL RIGHT?
!
TH-THERE ARE TWO MIKIS...
DID HE...
DID HE DO ANYTHING TO YOU?

I'M HIS TWIN!
KOZUE...
WHAT?
YOU'RE HIS SISTER?
YOU SURE LOOK ALIKE!
WOW...
NICE TO MEET YOU! I'M UTENA TENJOU!
DON'T TOUCH THAT! MY BRACELET-- IT'S A SET WITH MIKI'S!

THE STUDENT COUNCIL PRESIDENT **WARNED** ME...
...THAT THERE'S A GIRL **SEDUCING** MY BROTHER!
THAT'S WHY I'VE COME TO **SAVE** HIM.
TOUGA...?
I'VE ALWAYS BEEN WITH MIKI--EVER SINCE WE WERE BORN.
THAT'S WHY I KNOW **EVERYTHING** ABOUT HIM... CAN FEEL THINGS EVEN WHEN WE'RE APART.
KOZUE!
HE WOULD ONLY LIKE SOMEONE **I** WOULD LIKE.
THAT'S HOW WE ARE!
THIS TWIN THING...
...MUST BE A ROYAL PAIN.

GOOD LUCK! ♡
...EVEN THOUGH HE'S SO TOTALLY CUTE AND POPULAR!
...THE POOR GUY CAN'T MAKE ANY GIRLFRIENDS...
THEY SAY THAT'S WHY...
IS THAT SO?
AW!
Shoo Shoo
KOZUE...
I KNOW HOW SHE FEELS.
...BUT FEEL SOME ENVY.
I CAN'T HELP...
YEP!
MIKI'S LI'L SIS...
...IS FAMOUS FOR HAVING A SUPER DUPER BROTHER COMPLEX!

...CAN BE AWFULLY NICE.
HAVING A BIG BROTHER...
ANTHY ... YOU HAVE A BIG BROTHER?
Wow! She TALKED!
I'VE NEVER SEEN ANTHY LOOK... SO HAPPY.
YES...
ALTHOUGH I HARDLY EVER GET TO SEE HIM...

SURE, WE LIVE TOGETHER--BUT I STILL KNOW ***NOTHING*** ABOUT ANTHY'S PRIVATE LIFE!
NOW I'LL HAND BACK THE MATH QUIZ.
ARGH
BELOW A 40, AND YOU TAKE IT AGAIN!
GAK!
38
CLASS 2-A
NAME Utena Tenjou
I GUESS I'M TAKING THE MAKEUP IN A FEW DAYS...

I'VE NEVER HAD TO TAKE MAKEUPS IN MATH, DAMMIT! JUST BEEN SO BUSY...
WITH DUELS AND SUCH.
HMM. IS THAT A FACT?

YOU DON'T CARE! I'M SURE YOU GOT A GOOD GRADE...
ME? NOT AT ALL.
FWSH

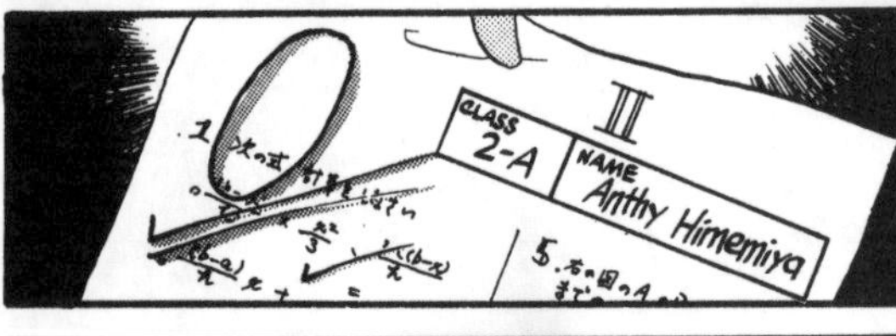
II
CLASS
2-A
NAME
Anthy Himemiya

ZERO...
For real?
I ALWAYS TAKE THE MAKEUPS.

I DON'T LET THEM BOTHER ME.

ANTHY... SHE LIVES ON A GREATER SCALE THAN THE REST OF US...
FWUP

38...
ACK!!
UTENA TENJOU GOT A 38--
HEY--
FWAP

MIKI?!

I-- I JUST HAPPENED TO PICK IT UP!
REALLY!
COULD I HAVE THAT BACK?
I HAVE TO TAKE IT OVER.
HMMM

HOLD ON.
KLIK
SKRATCHA SKRATCHA
OKAY.
THESE ARE THE RIGHT ANSWERS.

WOW...
YOU **ARE** A GENIUS. THESE ARE SEVENTH GRADE QUESTIONS...
...AND YOU DID THEM SO ***EASILY***...

I CAN SHOW YOU WHAT TO STUDY.
I HAVE A PRETTY GOOD IDEA...
...WHAT WILL BE ON THE TEST.

SURE.
YOU MEAN IT?
ISN'T THAT GREAT?
ANTHY, MIKI CAN COME OVER TO OUR ROOM AND...
ANTHY?

I'LL BE THERE, TOO.
WHY DON'T YOU STUDY IN OUR ROOM?

Student Council House 2
RIGHT, MIKI?
...I GUESS.

...SO THEN YOU SUBSTITUTE THAT HERE.
Y GOES THERE. ...
AND THEN YOU FACTOR ...
EEP!
7TH GRADE STUFF IS WAY BEYOND ME!
ENOUGH!
WE'VE BEEN GOING AT IT FOR TWO HOURS!
LET'S TAKE A BREAK!
Phew
FWMP
KOZUE, COULD YOU GET US SOME TEA?
SURE.
YOU'RE SUCH A GOOD TEACHER, MIKI.
I FEEL LIKE I'M GUARANTEED A 100 THIS TIME...
AW, I'M NOT ALL THAT...

NO... REALLY ...
.....
ZZHH

...HUH?
WHAT IS IT, MIKI?
...MMM.

WHAT WAS I...
I DOZED OFF FOR A SECOND, I GUESS.
SHE SAW ME...
ARE YOU OKAY?
Oh no, THE TEA... LET ME HELP...
SPLEEEESH
WHAT...
WERE YOU... JUST DOING TO HIM?
HRRMPH

WAP!
KOZUE, STOP IT...
WHAT ARE YOU--?
DON'T PLAY ALL SWEET AND INNOCENT WITH ME! NOT DRESSED LIKE THAT!
...YOU KNOW IT'S NOT RIGHT...
...TO GO AND BLAME UTENA.
NOT WHEN IT WAS ME...

WHAT?!
SO GO ON. BLAME ME.
I WAS THE ONE...
...WHO KISSED HER WHILE SHE SLEPT.
WE'RE NOT A SINGLE ENTITY ANYMORE!
WE FALL IN LOVE WITH DIFFERENT PEOPLE...LEAD DIFFERENT LIVES...
IT'S BETTER THAT WAY... FOR BOTH OF US.
I LIKE HER--AND THAT'S ALL THAT COUNTS.
DON'T YOU SEE, KOZUE?
SPEAK FOR YOURSELF, TRAITOR!
"BOTH OF US"?!

SLAM
Phew
LET'S GET BACK TO WORK.
.....

TO HIT YOUR SISTER ...
TO MAKE HER CRY...
YOU KNOW ...
...IT'S NOT LIKE YOU...
MIKI LIKES ME?

I-I'M SORRY.
.....

THAT'S NOT THE PROBLEM!
NEXT TIME I KISS YOU...
...I'LL BE SURE AND GET YOUR PERMISSION FIRST.

HIC
HOW COULD HE...
SOB
HOW COULD HE HIT ME LIKE THAT?
HOW COULD HE DO THIS TO ME?
THE GIRLFRIEND MATTERS MORE THAN THE SISTER, OF COURSE.
EVEN IF THEY'RE TWINS.
WHO MATTERS MORE-- ME OR UTENA?

Shhh... POOR KOZUE...
KOZUE?
KOZUE ...
ARE YOU ASLEEP?
UTENA'S GOING HOME.
TAP TAP
I'M SORRY ABOUT BEFORE...
Student Council H

.....
SHE'S STILL NOT BACK YET?
IT'S SORT OF LATE...
THE ROSE SEAL...
!
FWISH
Raging winds shall strip the leaves from the young treetop...
KOZUE
WITH THE LETTER-- IT'S KOZUE'S BRACELET...
?!

...unless you act. Tonight.
On the day of Tiu, when the bell strikes midnight...
...cross swords with the one who stands beneath the inverted castle--and triumph.
Cross swords...
...and triumph.
HUH? WHERE'S KOZUE?
CLUNK
KOZUE...

BUT WHY? BY WHOM? FOR WHAT?
I DON'T KNOW-- BUT I'M GOING!
YOUR SISTER'S BEEN KIDNAPPED?
THEN I'M GOING, TOO!
I-I DON'T WANT YOU TO SEE ME DO THIS!
YOU KNOW I BELIEVE DUELING IS WRONG, UTENA...
YOU LOOK REALLY COOL RIGHT NOW...
BUT WHY NOT?

LOOK-- UP AT THE TOP!
SOMEONE'S THERE ...!
...STRONG, COURAGEOUS, VALIANT...
...READY TO PROTECT YOUR ONLY SISTER!

ANTHY? WHY ARE YOU HERE...?
DID YOU KIDNAP MY SISTER?
PMSH
...A LETTER WITH THE ROSE SEAL DELIVERED TO THE DORM.
FOR YOU, LADY UTENA...

.....
TONIGHT. ON THE DAY OF TIU...
WHEN THE BELL STRIKES MIDNIGHT...
...CROSS SWORDS WITH THE ONE WHO STANDS BENEATH THE INVERTED CASTLE...
THE ROSE SEAL...?
WITH MIKI...?
!
WITH UTENA...
GONNNG
GONNNG
GONG

MIKI KAROU...
THE MIDNIGHT BELL ON THE DAY OF TIU, THE GOD OF WAR, SHALL BEGIN THE DUEL...
...YOU *WILL*...
...WANT TO DUEL!
--BY THE RULES OF THE ROSE SEAL!
WE MUST LIVE--WE MUST *FIGHT*--

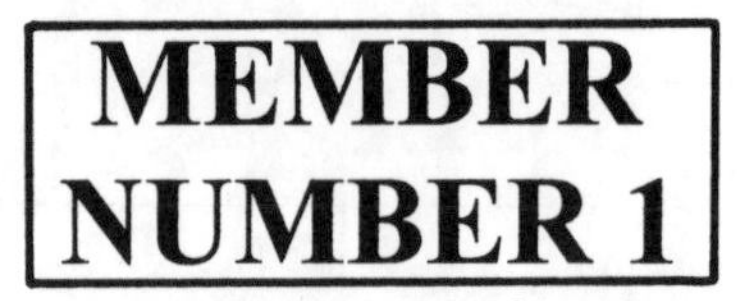

UTENA TENJOU

AGE: 14
BIRTHDAY: December 29th
SIGN: Capricorn
BLOOD TYPE: B
HEIGHT: 164cm (5'4")
WEIGHT: 46kg (101 lbs.)

HOBBIES: Any sport!
Collecting rose teacups ♡
Dressing like a tomboy!

TALENTS: Giving piggyback rides
(when forced by Wakaba...)

DISLIKES: Fermented Soybeans (Natto)
Guys who are clingy

Once upon a time, when Utena became an anime, Mr. Ikuhara the director came to ask...

And to this day, the anime Utena has a black uniform!

A DUEL... BETWEEN ME AND MIKI?!

AND I MUST WIN THE DUEL--OR LOSE KOZUE...
Oh, MY SISTER...
THIS IS TOO CRUEL!
TOUGA KIRYUU?
THE ROSE THAT TAKES FLIGHT FROM WORLD'S END...
...FOR YOU...
IT'S...
...IT'S A TRAP! SOMEONE WANTS US...
BUT WHO?
...TO TURN AGAINST EACH OTHER.
THE SMALL ROSE WITHIN ME...
FOR YOU...
ANTHY...

...UTENA?
YES... IT'S A TRAP.
FINISH
BUT I WON'T BE TAKEN IN...

I'LL LOSE FOR YOU, MIKI.
...THAT'S WHY...
IT'S THE ONLY WAY...
...TO GET KOZUE BACK FOR YOU...
...LADY UTENA.
WH... WHAT?

DON'T WORRY, ANTHY...
MIKI'S A NICE GUY...
I'M SURE HE'LL TAKE GOOD CARE OF YOU...
You and ChuChu.

YOU'RE THE ONE... WHO'S REALLY NICE.

UTENA...
NOW THEN!
LET'S GET ON WITH IT!

MIKI!!
YOU FORGOT THIS!
WANG
!
...YES... TOUGA?
DAMN YOU, TOUGA KIRYUU!

DON'T YOU WANT TO SEE IT THROUGH-- TO THE BITTER END?
TO SEE THE POWER OF DIOS, THE POWER TO REVOLUTIONIZE THE WORLD?
THIS MAY BE WHAT YOU PREDICTED, BUT...

THROW THE MATCH...
...AND YOU'RE NO PRINCE!
AND YOU NEVER GET TO SEE YOUR PRINCE, EITHER...
.....
I...

SO IT WAS YOU WHO SET THIS UP...!
H-HOW DO YOU...?!
YOU KNOW...
KOZUE WON'T COME BACK UNLESS YOU TWO FIGHT FOR REAL.
RMB
?!
M-MY PRINCE...
OOO!

WHAT?
RMB RMB RMB RMB RMB
IT IS THE POWER...
FLASH
AN EARTH-QUAKE?

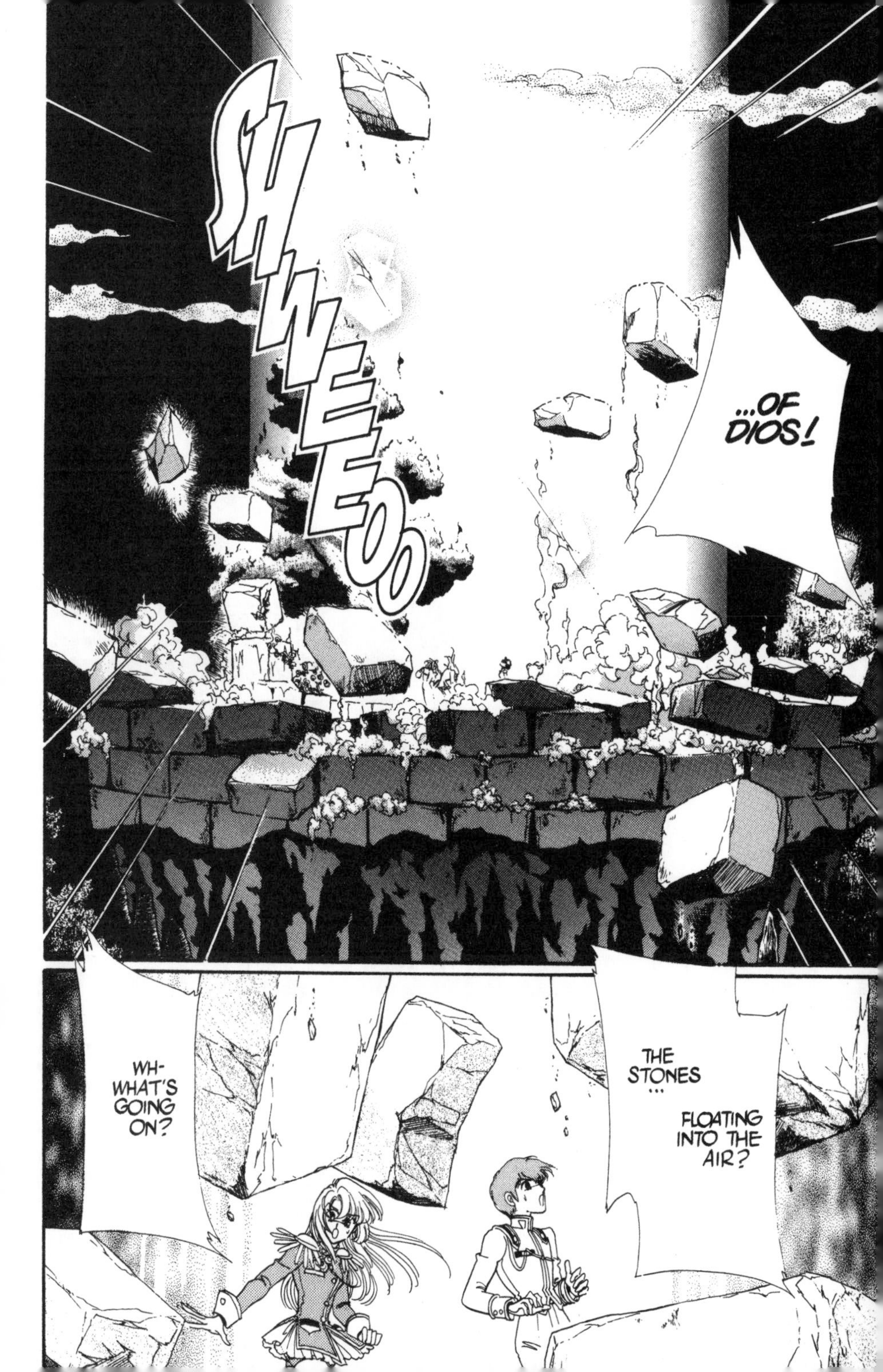
SHWEEEOO
...OF DIOS!
THE STONES ...
FLOATING INTO THE AIR?
WH-WHAT'S GOING ON?

UP TOWARD THE PALACE IN THE SKY...
MIKI...
HELP ME!
!

NOW LISTEN UP...
UNLESS YOU ACTIVATE THE POWER OF DIOS, KOZUE WON'T BE ABLE TO GET DOWN. SO TELL ME, UTENA TENJOU...
KOZUE ...

!
I...
LET'S DO IT.
...WILL YOU RISK IT?
CAN YOU *STILL* LOSE ON PURPOSE?
MIKI...
LET'S FIGHT WITHOUT HOLDING BACK.
IT'S MY DUEL...
...I CAN BE STRONG...
IT'S OKAY.
UTENA, I WON'T LOSE.

ALL RIGHT.
.....
HYAH!

KTANG
KLANNG
Yah!
Hah!
I AM... THE ROSE BRIDE...
...I?
Hmm?
WHICH ONE...
...DO YOU WANT TO WIN?
MIKI...

HFF
UFF
I SHALL FOLLOW THE VICTOR...
...YOU REALLY ARE STRONG!
MIKI...
...BY THE LAW OF THE ROSE SEAL.
MY SISTER'S LIFE IS RIDING ON IT.
I WON'T LOSE, EVEN TO YOU.

I MUST HAVE THE STRENGTH...
...TO FORCE YOU TO GIVE IT YOUR ALL!
UNGH!

MATANG
AND I WON'T LOSE...
...NOT EVEN TO YOU!
Uhn!
I'LL SEE IT THROUGH...

WH-- WHAT...
...IS THIS LIGHT ...?

MIKI!
ZLASH

AND UTENA TENJOU WINS THE DUEL.

MIKI, I...
I WON?

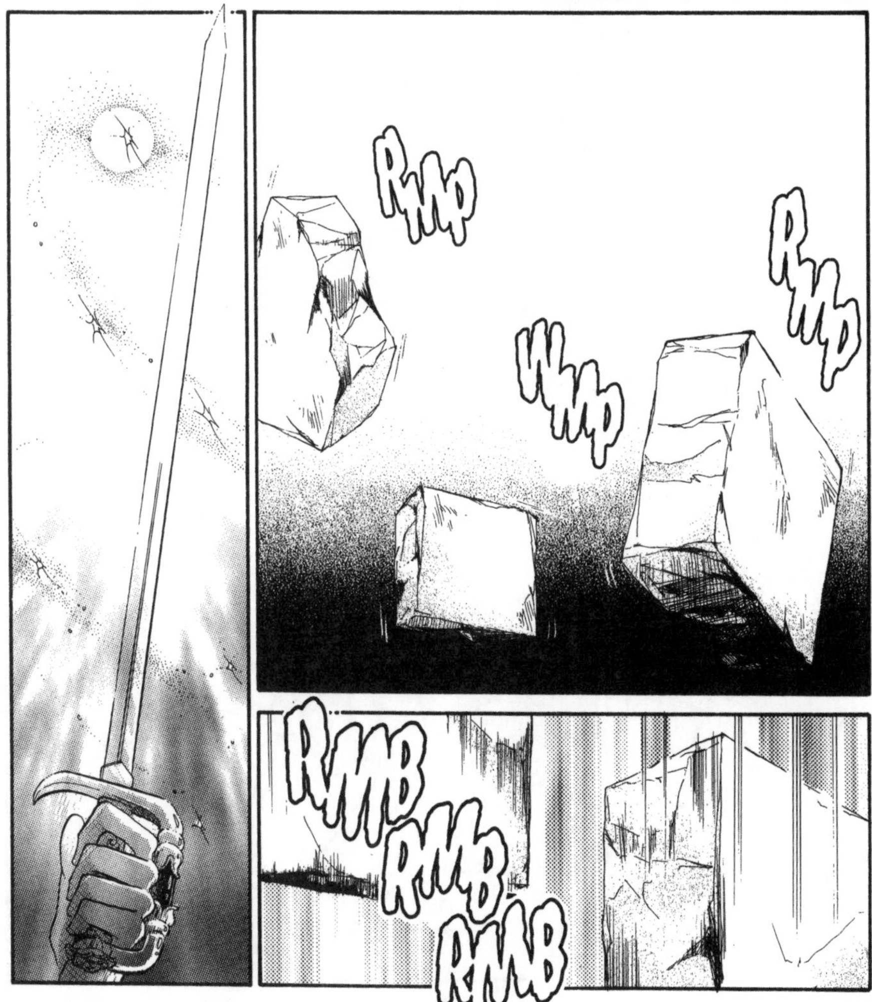
RMP
RMP
WMP
RMB
RMB
RMB

YAAH!
WUMP
oof
FLISH
?
KOZUE...
MIKI... I'M SORRY!
SORRY I MADE YOU DO THIS...
I WON'T EVER...
...EVER DO IT AGAIN!
!
WHSSHHH

ANTHY HIMEMIYA TOLD ME TO FOLLOW HER...
...THAT SHE COULD SHOW ME...
...WHO MY BROTHER TRULY LOVED...

I'M SORRY! I'M SO SORRY, MIKI...
I WAS SO WORRIED-- THAT IF YOU GOT HURT, IT WOULD BE MY FAULT.
ANTHY LED KOZUE?

MIKI!
IT'S OKAY.
I'M JUST GLAD YOU'RE BACK SAFE.

LADY UTENA!
FMP

ANTHY...
WHY DID YOU DO THIS?
HOW IS YOUR HAND?
WE SHOULD CLEAN IT...
YEAH...

SOON.
YOU'LL SEE YOUR PRINCE SOON.

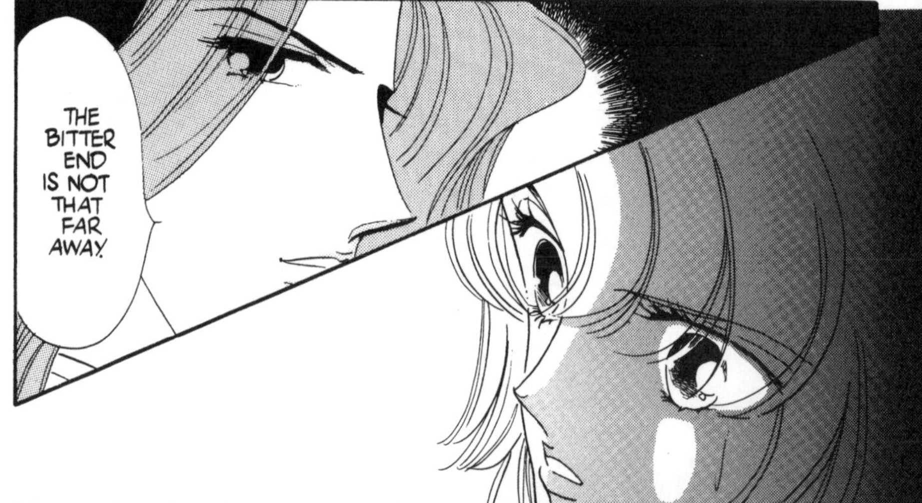
THE BITTER END IS NOT THAT FAR AWAY.

TOUGA KIRYUU!
WHAT DO YOU KNOW THIS TIME?
TELL ME! C'MON!
TELL ME!
YEAH... THANKS.
I'M GLAD IT WASN'T A SERIOUS WOUND.
IT'LL BE A BIT INCONVENIENT FOR DAILY TASKS, I'M AFRAID...

..BUT WE HAVE A FRIEND TO HELP OUT!
YEAH... BY THE WAY, ANTHY...
I NEED TO ASK YOU--
CHUCHU, ARE YOU DONE?
Chuuu
Chu!

HIS HOOP'S FROM A CANDY BOX!
SO I MADE HIM A NECKTIE TO MATCH MINE!
I FELT SORRY FOR HIM, BEING NAKED ALL THE TIME...
DOESN'T IT LOOK GOOD ON HIM?
.....

Hmm.
I DUNNO-- IT SEEMS TO ACCENTUATE HIS NUDITY MORE THAN HIDE IT...
REALLY? YOU THINK SO?
ANTHY...

DID YOU DO IT?
DID YOU TELL KOZUE TO PRETEND...
...THAT SHE'D BEEN KID-NAPPED?

I WON'T GET MAD.
ANTHY, I PROMISE YOU...
I JUST NEED...
...I JUST NEED TO HEAR THE **TRUTH** FROM YOU.

.....
I AM THE ROSE BRIDE...

...SO I WILL DO WHATEVER YOU **SAY.**
BUT THAT'S NOT **IT,** ANTHY!
I WANT YOU TO ANSWER AS A **FRIEND.**

...AS A... AS A **FRIEND?**

...YOU MEAN THAT...
...YOU... AND I...
LADY UTENA...
ALL RIGHT.
JUST ANSWER MY QUESTIONS.
YOU COULDN'T POSSIBLY HAVE SET UP THE DUEL, RIGHT?
...YES.
SOMEONE ORDERED YOU TO BRING KOZUE, RIGHT?
YES.

WAS IT... TOUGA KIRYUU ...?
Gulp

...A LETTER WITH THE ROSE SEAL! YOU KNOW I CANNOT DISOBEY THE WILL OF WORLD'S END.
I, TOO, WAS SENT A LETTER...
SO WORLD'S END WOULD THINK NOTHING OF TOYING WITH US...?!

Miss Utena Tenjou
UNTIL LAST YEAR...
...THE ONLY LETTERS WITH THE ROSE SEAL SENT TO ME...
...SMELLED OF ROSES...
...AND BROUGHT NEWS AND ENCOURAGE-MENT FROM MY PRINCE...
Hall
Chu!
TIP TUP TIP
LADY UTENA!
IT'S HERE-- ONE MORE...
Oh...
Miss Utena Tenjou
Papoom

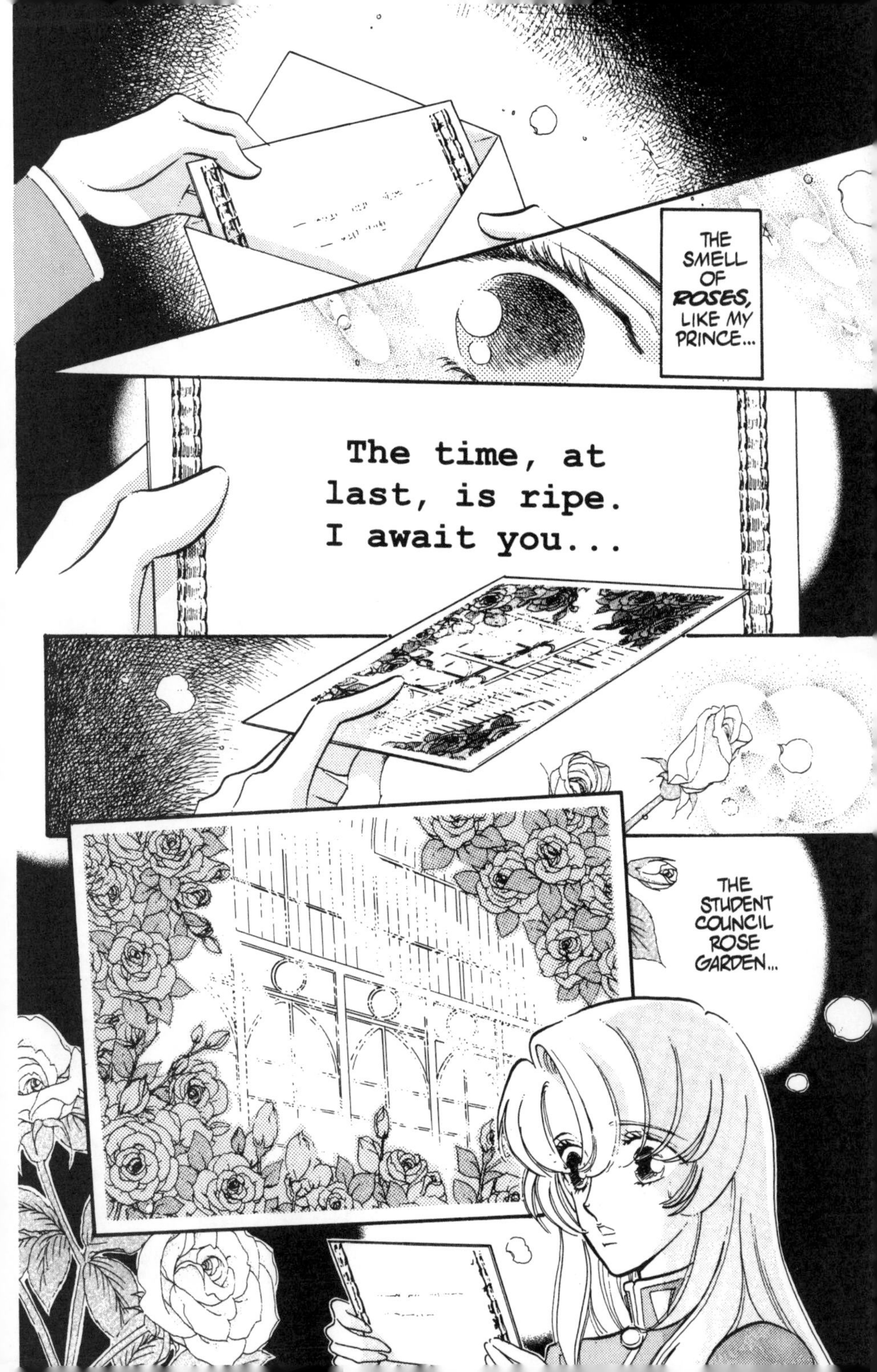
THE SMELL OF ROSES, LIKE MY PRINCE...
The time, at last, is ripe. I await you...
THE STUDENT COUNCIL ROSE GARDEN...

FINALLY!

THE PRINCE THAT I'VE BEEN ***WAITING*** FOR...

IT COULDN'T BE...!
NO...

SLAM!

THERE YOU ARE...
UTENA TENJOU.
I AM HERE...
YOUR PRINCE.
TOUGA...
KIRYUU!

TO BE CONTINUED IN
VOLUME 3: TO SPROUT

TEAM UTENA
MEMBER NUMBER 2

ANTHY HIMEMIYA

AGE:	14
BIRTHDAY:	February 29
SIGN:	Pisces
BLOOD TYPE:	AB
HEIGHT:	157cm (5'1")
WEIGHT:	41kg (90lbs)
HOBBIES:	Playing cards Playing with animals
LIKES:	Talking with animals
DISLIKES:	Studying Cooking Making friends

WHEN UTENA BECAME AN ANIME, MR. IKUHARA THE DIRECTOR SAID...

...AND SO THE ANIME ANTHY WEARS RED.

To Curry Favor

I'm Chuchu...
A knight who protects the princess, Anthy Himemiya...
MONKEY!
ANTHY IS MY BRIDE.
OUT OF THE WAY!
The hateful Saionji!
But...
...a strong prince chased Saionji away!
Now it's the three of us--
--the prince Utena Tenjou, my master, and me!
WIN

Oh, CHUCHU! HOW NAUGHTY!
ANTHY!
CHUCHU ATE MY SNACK AGAIN!
East Hall
I'm so happy when I'm full!
Snnzz zzzz
FAKER! YOU'RE NOT ASLEEP!
I HEARD THAT YOU LIKE CURRY, LADY UTENA.
I'M SORRY, LADY UTENA.
I'LL MAKE YOU SOME-THING INSTEAD.
WHAT?
YOU CAN COOK, ANTHY?!
I'LL BE RIGHT BACK.
YEAH, BUT... FOR A SNACK?
Um!
SURE.
My master, cook-ing?
TIPTIPTIP
Oh, no!
bink!

CURRY, CURRY...
MIX ANY THING AND IT CAN BE CURRY!
PING
A TOUCH OF FLAVOR!
GMP
TMP
COCOA
RED PEPPER
MISO
CHEESE
A FEW VEGGIES!
CHOP
SPLUNK
SPLUNK
SPIP
SPAP
MAYO

SWP
GASP!
MMMM!
VERY NICE!
TWMP
SLURP

Gah!
It's awful... the worst!

I can't let Lady Utena eat this!
What should I do...?!
TIPTUPTIPTUP
Chili Sauce
Chu!
Lady Utena! Your snack is ready!
KATON
Kick-yo-ass hot!
Fire Curry
100TH POWER

I'll hide the taste with some heat.

PISH PASH

A bit more...

SPURSH

BLUB BLUB
BLUB BLUB BLUB
What should I do?!
WOW, IT SMELLS GOOD.
CHUCHU?
Chu!
VROOMMM!
I'VE NEVER BEEN SO FAMISHED!
LET'S EAT!
WOW! PIPING HOT! YUM!
HISS
SSST
HERE YOU GO...

East Hall
KABOOM
East Hall
NOW WE CAN CHOW DOWN!

WEOO
WEOO
WEOO
WEOO
UTENA TENJOU?! ANTHY HIMEMIYA?!
DON'T THEY LIVE HERE?!
AN EXPLOSION IN THE EAST HALL?
WHAT'S GOING ON?!
TOUGA...
Um, STUDENT COUNCIL PRESIDENT...
WHO DID IT, AND FOR *WHAT?*
WHAT COULD HAVE CAUSED THIS?
THIS IS THE WORST CRISIS EVER TO BEFALL THE ROSE SEAL.
THE ROSE BRIDE AND HER BETROTHED-- SOMEONE PLANTED A *BOMB?*

THEY'RE BOTH OKAY. THE HOSPITAL RELEASED THEM.
Oh... WELL, GOOD.
YEAH.
BUT THEY'RE, uh...
BOTH A BIT WEIRD...
Nah... IT'S MY IMAGINATION.
HAS TO BE...
...I HOPE.
"WEIRD"?
GLOM
U-TE-NA! ARE YOU OKAY NOW?
I'M SO GLAD MY UTENA IS SAFE...

ANTHY.
U-
UTENA?
That's not like her.
FWUMP
WHAP
WHAT ARE YOU DOING?!
I'M GLAD-- I WAS WORRIED.
Chu!
CHMP

Something's wrong...
LET'S GO HOME.
ANTHY *ATTACKED* OUR DEAR SAIONJI...
I'M SORRY ABOUT ALL THIS.
U-UTENA?
...ANTHY?

WHAP
!
ANTHY HIMEMIYA! HOW DARE YOU?
TO HIT MY DEAR SAIONJI!
YOU KNOW WHAT YOU DESERVE?
TO BE ETERNALLY DANGLING FROM UTENA TENJOU'S BUTT, JUST LIKE GOLDFISH POOP!
My master's in trouble!

SLAM
CHUCHU!
WHAT'S WRONG!
Lady Utena, please do something!
Chu!
Help!
Chu!
Help!
Chu!
...AND ANTHY IS LADY UTENA.
I'M ANTHY...
CHUCHU, IT'S OKAY.
Huh?

HOW DARE YOU DEFY US, PUNY ANTHY HIMEMIYA...
WHAT ARE YOU DOING?
SO THAT'S HOW IT IS...
Wha...
What's going on?
...POOR THING... TO PUT UP WITH SUCH ABUSE...
I GUESS FOR ANTHY IT'S ALWAYS LIKE THIS...
DAY IN AND DAY OUT...
GLOMP
!

SORRY.
I THINK YOU GIRLS HAVE A *LESSON* TO LEARN.
THIS IS FROM THE *BOTH* OF US--
FOR ALL YOUR BULLY-ING.
KASWAP!

YOU'RE SO COOL!
Oh, ANTHY!
EEP...
WH-WHAT?
IT'S U-UTENA!
SHE'S EVEN SCARIER.
EEK
UTENA!
RUN!

I'M SORRY, LADY UTENA.
IT LOOKED LIKE **I** HAD PAID THEM BACK...
AND IT FELT SO GOOD...
AND I NEED TO APOLOGIZE FOR MAKING ***YOUR*** BODY GET ALL ***VIOLENT,*** ANTHY.
I'LL BE CARE-FUL...
...FROM NOW ON.
Umm?! Uhhh...
CHUCHU!
CHECK THIS OUT!
OUR PERSONALITIES GOT SWITCHED IN THE EXPLOSION!
So my master is...

BLACK

So Anthy is Utena...
urk!
...and Utena is Anthy?

WHY DID THIS HAPPEN?
I DON'T MIND STAYING THIS WAY...
I *LIKE* SEEING ANTHY BE COOL LIKE THAT.
WELL, *I* MIND.
Saionji hugged me.
SOME-THING CAUSED THIS.
IT MUST HAVE BEEN...

THE CURRY!
ANTHY, MAKE IT THE SAME AS YOU DID LAST TIME!
OKAY!

Because of the explosion...
Because of the curry...
Because Chuchu put that stuff in!

I'll make things right!
I'll get them back to normal!
All I need is another explosion with that 100th power curry.
MART
SHWUP
CAN I HELP YOU?
Chu.
OUT ON AN ERRAND?
WHAT A CLEVER LITTLE MONKEY!
WHAT DO YOU NEED? Oh!
YOU WANT THE 100th POWER CURRY THAT WAS THERE?
BOING
WE JUST SOLD OUT.
KRESHHH

THE LAST ONE...
...SOLD IT JUST A MINUTE AGO...
LITTLE MONKEY, ARE YOU OKAY?
...six months...
IT'S A RARE ITEM--WE SHOULD HAVE MORE IN ABOUT SIX MONTHS.
SO YOU REALLY SEEM TO WANT THIS CURRY POWDER, eh?
Saionji!
MONKEY!
SQUASH
WUMP
Fire Curry
100
Chu!

Argh.
WELL LOOKY HERE!
WHUSH
SMUSH!
I COULD GIVE IT TO YOU...
...IF YOU DO WHAT I SAY.
.....
I'M GLAD YOU CAME TO ME...
ANTHY.

WE WERE TORN APART BY UTENA TENJOU...
...BUT *TODAY* IS OUR WEEKLY RECONFIRMATION OF OUR LOVE FOR ONE ANOTHER.
HUH?
L-LOVE...?
Please bear with it, Lady Utena!
WHY...
...WHAT DO YOU *MEAN?*
YOU DIDN'T TELL ME *THIS*, CHUCHU!
NOW *YOU* SHOW *ME*... SHOW ME YOUR *LOVE!*
!
I'LL *SHOW* YOU HOW MUCH I LOVE YOU.
LOOK, ANTHY. LOOK!
WSH

ANTHY!
WHOA, NOT AGAIN...
SHWAP
GAWOMP
CHUCHU, I'M SORRY!
I DIDN'T MEAN TO HIT YOU...
Chu...
It's okay... I sacrificed myself of my own free will...
MMMMooo
I'M ENAMORED OF HOW FEISTY YOU'VE GOTTEN RECENTLY.

HERE IT IS...
THE USUAL ...MY LOVE TO YOU.
PWAP
I'LL BE WAITING TO HEAR OF YOUR LOVE FOR ME.
MONKEY, I'LL FULFILL OUR PROMISE--
--WHEN YOU BRING THAT BACK!
.....
Kyouichi Saionji
Love Forever
Anthy Himemiya
AN EX-CHANGE DIARY...
...SOME SORT OF SLAM BOOK OF LOVE?!

YOU'VE BEEN KEEPING THIS UP ALL ALONG?
Saturday
I am resigned to only writing of our love for now, but I will continue my sword training and get you back someda
You must wait f
ANTHY, I DON'T **BELIEVE** IT...
DON'T GIVE ME THAT!
WHY SHOULD **I** WRITE TO THAT PERVERT?
YOU'RE ANTHY RIGHT NOW, LADY UTENA.
THEN **YOU** WRITE THE RESPONSE.
YES.
SAIONJI INSISTED ON IT.
Chu!
Chu!
YOU'RE GOING TO WRITE IT, CHUCHU?

I look just like her!
Chuchu will get you back to normal...
I'm sorry, you two...
Snff-chu!
Oh, THANK YOU!
WE'RE BOTH SO TIRED FROM MAKING CURRY ALL THE TIME.
Sorry!
It just wouldn't explode.
HERE YOU GO.
YOUR REWARD.
HMM...
LOOKS LIKE YOU BROUGHT THE RESPONSE BACK.
fip fap

The 100th power curry power!
Sigh-chu!
SMAK
Fire Curry
Kick-yo-ass-hot!
100TH POWER
I did it!
VROOM
WOW... THAT WAS FAST.
WHAT'S THE MONKEY SO HAPPY ABOUT?
ZWIP
...
WH-WHAT IS THIS...?

HE MUST HAVE WRITTEN THIS!
Chu
Chu
Anthy
Chu
My dear Saionji
I'm sorry this is so late. Today I'll rite about Anthy's favorite foods.
•Banana
•And Cookies
•And Sweet Pota
•Apples
THAT DAMNED MONKEY...
YEAH.
CURRY AGAIN
... EAT UP.
...
Hall
WHAT?
CHUCHU!
SLAM

BANG
STOP IT! WHAT ARE YOU POURING ON US?
BING
CHUCHU, WHAT ARE YOU DOING?
BOING
...BUT I WILL BE AVENGED!
FNSHA
KOFF KOFF
CHUCHU, WHY ARE YOU...
100TH POWER CURRY POWDER?
SAIONJI...
YOU CHEATED ME OUT OF MY 100TH POWER CURRY POWDER...
MONKEY!
YOU LIED TO ME!
URK

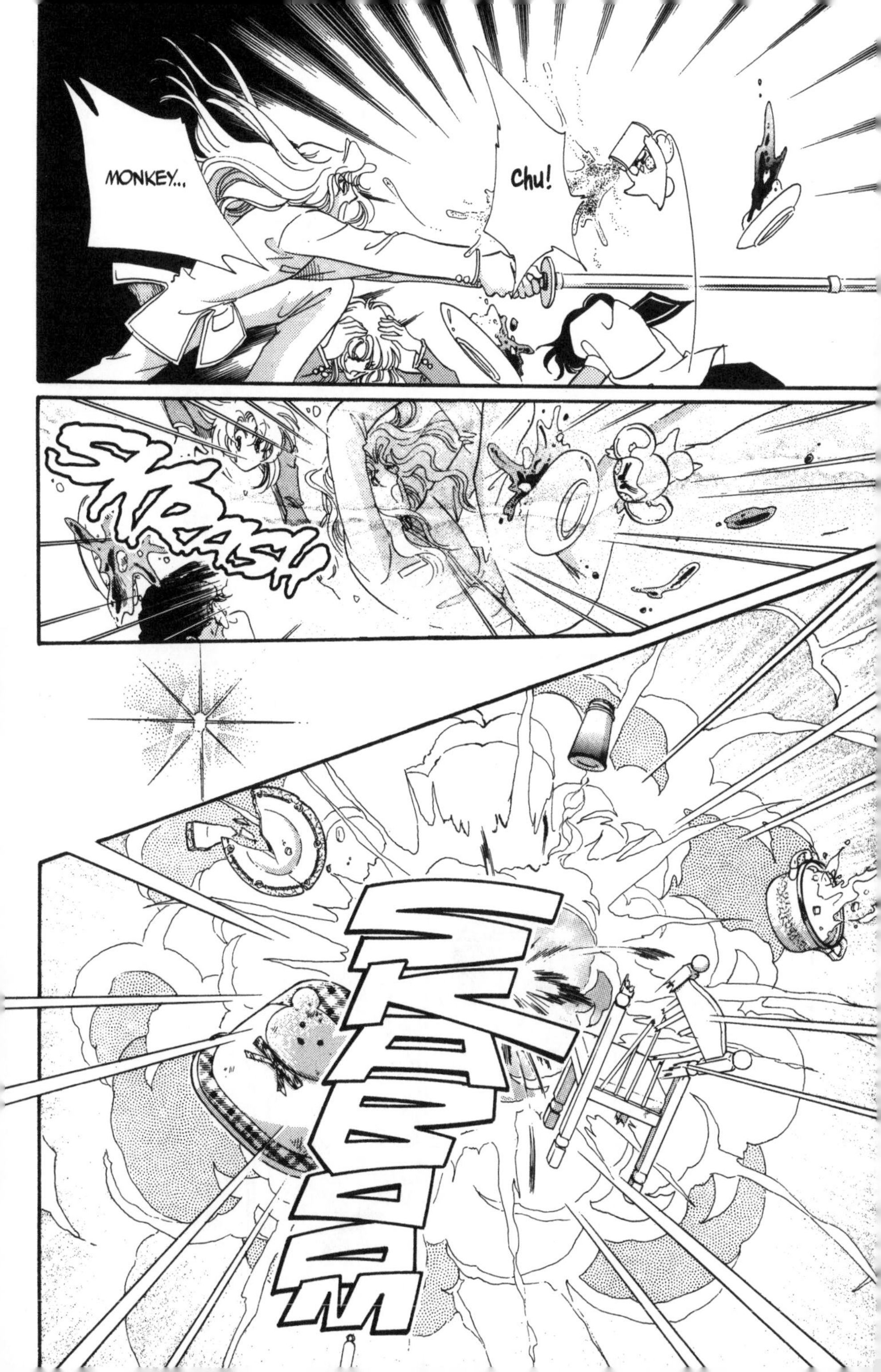
MONKEY...
Chu!
SPLASH
SMASH

ANOTHER BOMB IN THE EAST HALL...
Oh, NO...
Chu?
Twitch
Unh...
Oh...

WE DID IT!
WE'RE BACK TO NORMAL, LADY UTENA.
Oh...
LADY... UTENA?
DAMMIT, WHAT THE HELL...
eep!
CHUCHU!
CHUCHU!
YOU'RE SUCH A BAD BOY!
THE CURRY POWDER DID IT, RIGHT?!
THE FIRST EXPLOSION WAS YOUR FAULT, TOO!
YAY!
...BUT THAT MEANS...

Chu.
Chu!
Chu!
Chu!
...chu?
Chu...
Chu!
Chu!
UM
CHUCHU!
YOU WON'T TALK YOUR WAY OUT OF *THIS* ONE!

YEAH, YEAH...
SAIONJI!
WERE THE GIRLS OKAY?
THE EAST HALL!
COME HELP!
OUR PERSON-ALITIES--
SWITCHED IN THAT EXPLOSION!
TRAPPED IN SAIONJI'S BODY...
...BUT IT'S BETTER THAN A SCOLDING!

Chu!
GOTTA RUN!
TO CURRY FAVOR:
THE END

It's been so long that I've forgotten what started it, but when I was in elementary school, there was a class-sized afternoon "battle" in a vacant lot with the students from a neighboring school. I don't remember the outcome, so it couldn't have been much of a "battle." But at the time, I felt a strange uplift—a feeling of fulfillment (sad to say) that I remember distinctly. I wonder what it means.

CHIHO SAITO

I took up Kendo when I was in Jr. high. I should say I tried to take it up because I was terrible—I lost nearly every match I entered. I wondered why I was so bad at this form of competition, and one thought would resound in my mind, "I want to be good at this!" I think that maybe Utena's duels stem from my old Kendo obsession.

KUNIHIKO IKUHARA

BE PAPAS:

A group of highly creative people founded by director Kunihiko Ikuhara (Sailor Moon, Schell Bullet) and including such storied members as master manga artist Chiho Saito (Kakan no Madonna, Lady Masquerade) and animator Shinya Hasegawa (Evangelion). Their collaboration produced the Utena TV series and the movie, Revolutionary Girl Utena: The Adolescence of Utena, and recently they have produced a new work called The World of S&M.

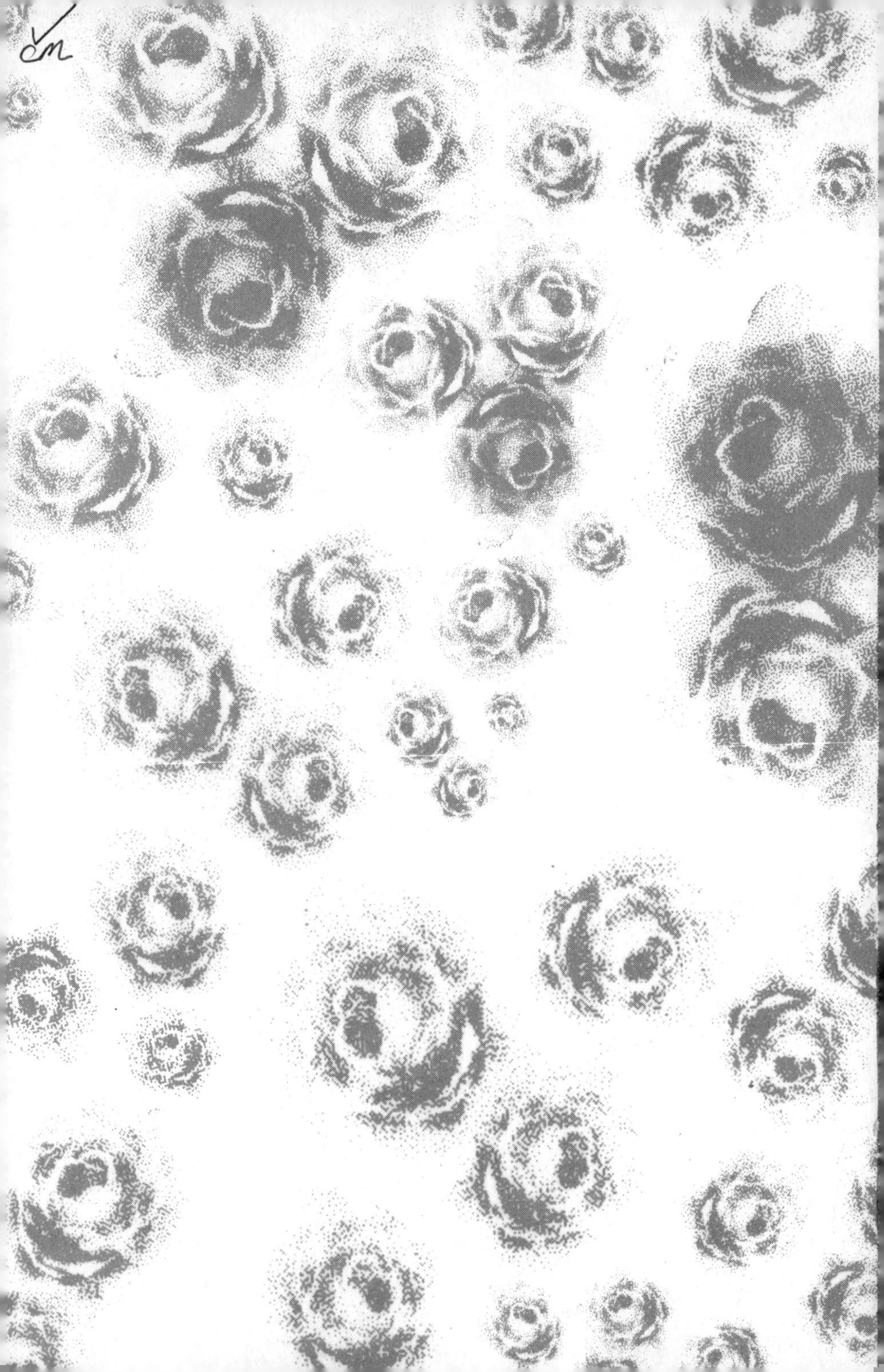